"Oh, damn! You're . . ."

The girl's look of smug delight was answer enough.

It hadn't occurred to Dex until that precise moment that *this* was the widow Wilhelmina Stout.

"And what, may I ask, sir, is of such life-and-death importance that you must speak with me?"

"I, uh . . ." Dex was given a moment to reflect on how much and how honestly he should explain.

James had his hat in his hands and a look of interest in his eyes. But then the girl was certain to have that effect on any red-blooded male between the ages of, roughly, puberty and three days after death.

Dex stood. "This is the friend and partner I was telling you about. James, this lady is Wilhelmina Stout."

James blinked.

"Now, gentlemen. What is that you've come here to tell me?"

"We came here to kill you," Dex blurted.

DIAMONDBACK

GAME OF CHANCE

◆ ◆ ◆

Guy Brewer

JOVE BOOKS, NEW YORK

This is a work of fiction. Names, characters, places, and incidents are
either the product of the author's imagination or are used fictitiously,
and any resemblance to actual persons, living or dead, business
establishments, events, or locales is entirely coincidental.

GAME OF CHANCE

A Jove Book / published by arrangement with
the author

PRINTING HISTORY
Jove edition / May 2000

The Penguin Putnam Inc. World Wide Web site address is
http://www.penguinputnam.com

ISBN: 0-515-12806-6

A JOVE BOOK®
Jove Books are published by The Berkley Publishing Group,
a division of Penguin Putnam Inc.,
375 Hudson Street, New York, New York 10014.
JOVE and the "J" design
are trademarks belonging to Penguin Putnam Inc.

PRINTED IN THE UNITED STATES OF AMERICA

10 9 8 7 6 5 4 3 2 1

DIAMONDBACK

GAME OF CHANCE

◆ ◆ ◆

• 1 •

"I have a present for you."

"Really? For what occasion?"

"For your birthday."

"My birthday isn't for another four months."

"That's close enough." She giggled and grinned. "Do you want to know when my birthday is?"

"Sure, honey."

"Today is my birthday."

"How old are you?"

"Nineteen." She fluttered her eyelashes outrageously, then laughed. He rather doubted that she was nineteen. Probably a good five years more. But then, who was counting? And this probably wasn't her birthday either. But who cared. He reached for the glass of brandy he'd brought up to the room with him.

"Do you have a present for me, honey?" The girl was not subtle. But she was cute. Surely that made up for it.

She said her name was Allison, and maybe it really was. Or not. That didn't matter either. What did matter was that she was dark-haired, dimple-cheeked and with a deliciously delicate body, all small bones and gentle curves. At least what he could see of it so far.

"I have this for you," he said, gesturing toward a bulge at the front of his trousers that threatened to pop buttons and take on a life of its own.

Allison's laughter was merry and sweet. Not innocent, mind. But definitely merry. "Sweetie, that's the kind of present I like the best," she declared with an impish wink and a wriggle of her hips.

"You can call me Dexter if you like," he said. "Or Dex for short."

"Dexter. I don't think I've ever known a fellow named Dexter before."

"Dexter Lee Yancey," he told her. "Late of Louisiana, now a citizen of the, um, world, shall we say."

"Me too, Dexter." Allison laughed again—he had no idea why—and wiggled some more. She looked cuter than ever when she did that. Which of course was probably why she did it. Allison was a young lady who knew which side the bread was buttered on. "You're cute, Dexter."

"Thanks." He'd had other girls say that and was always pleased to hear it, but hearing it nevertheless amazed him. In his own opinion he was decent looking but rather ordinary. At twenty-eight Dexter Yancey was a fit and lean man, an inch-and-a-bit under six feet in height, with dark blond hair and Burnside whiskers flowing down onto the shelf of a decently chiseled jaw. He had brown eyes and a ready smile, and thanks to rather a lot of travel by horseback in recent months he had developed something of a tan.

His clothing, and the way he carried himself in them, marked him as a gentleman. He favored light gray trousers, black stovepipe riding boots, a dark gray swallowtail coat and pearl gray planter's hat.

At the moment he'd laid aside his malacca walking stick with its ornate eagle-beak head.

"Don't you want to get more comfortable, Dexter honey? Like, I mean, you could take that big gun off." Allison gave him a dimpled smile. "That isn't the sort of gun you'll be needing right now."

"Of course." Dex shed his coat, vest and tie and took off

the heavy .455 Webley that rode in a crossdraw holster on the left side of his belly. Allison's eyes grew a tad wider when he also removed a previously hidden twin to the Webley from a springclip holster worn in the small of his back.

"Now this," Allison said, "is the gun I'm wanting to see." She stepped forward and laid a hand lightly onto the front of his britches. Her eyes became wider and her smile all the more merry. "Oh my. How nice. I hadn't realized what a big present you have for me."

Her fingers flew with the skill of much practice to help him finish undressing, and when she was done she clapped her hands with pleasure and bent to give his pecker a kiss on the red and ready tip. "Lovely," she said. "It's ever so pretty. The nicest birthday present I can remember."

That seemed to be gilding the lily a trifle overmuch, but Dex forgave her. She was angling for a tip over and above the negotiated cost of services, and all's fair in war and commerce. Or whatever that old saying was . . . or should have been.

"Can I get you anything, Dexter? More brandy?"

"You can take your clothes off and bring your pretty self over to this bed," Dex suggested as he stretched out and patted the sheet beside him.

The room, he was discovering, was surprisingly pleasant. The sheets were clean and smelled of soap and sunshine. The pillows were plump and the mattress firm. And of course there was Allison.

Dex smiled. A boy could scarcely ask for more than this.

The girl turned her back shyly and began a slow and rather enjoyable process of disrobing. Turning, posturing, teasing.

Dex laced his hands behind his neck and sighed, thoroughly admiring the artistry Allison put into the normally simple process of shedding her clothes. She made it seem practically an art form. Something that should be done on a lighted stage where throngs of happy fellows could admire the performance all at once.

Such a thing would never be allowed, though. The "de-

cent" elements of any town Dex ever heard of would be
sure to outlaw anything so salaciously tempting as that
would be. Out of sheer jealousy if for no other reason.

"You're smiling," Allison said. "What are you thinking
about?"

"Enjoying what I'm seeing," Dex told her. Which was
the truth, if not entirely all the truth.

She simpered, arched her back and with a twist of her
shoulders and a wiggle of her hips let the cloth of her dress
slide off her body, exposing the nicest playground Dex had
seen in many a day.

"Lovely," he said, meaning it most sincerely.

Allison laughed happily, quickly shucked herself out of
the remnants of clothing still blocking his view and with a
yip and a giggle came bouncing onto the bed to join him.

She was, he quickly determined, a delightful lass in all
the many ways that counted.

• 2 •

"Are we in the Nations yet?"

Dex shrugged. "To tell you the truth I'm not sure."

James scowled. "I swear, Dex, Texas reminds me somewhat of Hell. Except Texas is bigger. And hotter. And the people aren't as pleasant."

"You're prejudiced," Dex said with a laugh.

"Careful what you accuse me of, white boy. There's not a prejudiced bone in my fine and handsome body." James grinned, his very dark face cracking into a broad grin. James was a year younger than Dex and half an inch taller but otherwise almost looked like him. Almost. James was black. Once he had been Dex's slave, a living play toy. Dex had taken him everywhere, including to school, as a consequence of which James had an education the equal of nearly any southern planter's son and in fact much better than most.

Of course that knowledge had always been kept carefully away from both Dexter's late father and James's mother, neither of whom would have understood or approved of such a thing.

As for Dexter and James, they regarded it all as quite

normal and built a friendship that endured long past the "peculiar institution" of slavery.

"Anxious to get out of Texas, are you?"

James shuddered, not having to fake that at all in order to get his point across. Didn't have to remind Dex of just why he wanted out of Texas either. They'd recently incurred the undying wrath of a very rich young woman. Something to do with Dexter having killed her father. Justifiably, in his mind. Not so in hers.

She'd vowed to spend every one of the many cents she owned if that was what it took to gain revenge.

Dex had assumed that was merely the ranting of a distraught female, but lately they had on more than one occasion seen circulars posted in stores and trading posts along the way advertising a reward, no questions asked, for proof of Dexter's demise.

The posters bothered James considerably. Dex couldn't say that he exactly approved of them.

The only thing in their favor was that the circulars made no mention of Dex having a Negro traveling companion. But then Jane Carter would have attached no importance to the presence of a mere servant, as she surely would have assumed James to be. Thank goodness, Dex thought.

"You think we'll be shut of that woman once we get out of Texas?" James asked. He asked the same question roughly two times per hour and had been asking it ever since they saw the first reward poster.

Dex answered the exact same way he always did. "Damned if I'd know, James."

They had altered their planned direction of travel, and that was about all Dex knew to do. That and put some distance between them and Wharburton, Texas, on the Trinity River where the lovely Miss Carter waited like a spider overseeing its web.

Back in Wharburton they'd spoken of continuing west. To Austin, perhaps all the way on to far California. As soon as they realized Jane Carter was serious in her lust for revenge, they'd turned ninety degrees to the right and were looking for as quick an exit from inhospitable Texas as they could manage.

The Indian Territories, or so-called Indian Nations, presented their best and nearest hope for that. Of course neither of them knew exactly where the Nations were. Or what they could expect to find once they got there.

The point right now was simply to get there. Alive and unmolested.

Dex always hated to disappoint a lady. But then, what the hell. Jane Carter wasn't all that much a lady, and a little disappointment would hurt her a great deal less than pleasing her would hurt Dexter.

"I expect we can slow down and relax a little when we get to the next town," Dex said. "Surely she can't have papered the whole damn country with posters. Not this quick anyway."

"I hope you're right, because my butt is aching."

Dex gave his friend a searching look. James was still recovering from recent and rather serious injuries, and Dex suspected if he was willing to admit to a sore ass then the truth was that he was hurting almost bad enough to make him turn pale. And that would take an awful lot of hurting.

"We'll stop," Dex said firmly. "I'm betting it will be safe enough, whatever the next town is."

But then, not all bets pay off.

· 3 ·

Ki'iwa. That was what it looked like anyway. The hand-lettered sign had weathered, and whatever might once have been painted between the two i's was not legible now.

"Kiliwa?" James speculated aloud. "Kihiwa? Kitiwa?"

"Any one of them sounds as good as any other to me," Dex said. "Nothing I can think of makes any particular sense." He shrugged. "Could be they just put together the initials of whoever it was that started the place."

The town, whatever its name, wasn't exactly inspiring. It lay nested at the base of some lumpy and definitely *not* majestic . . . things . . . of stone and earth. In Dex's opinion these vertical protuberances were too large and ugly to be called hills but too small and spread out to be mountains. Not that he'd ever seen a mountain, exactly, they being rather thin on the ground in Louisiana. But he'd seen pictures. These things were not mountains.

In any event, the hills ran from southwest to northwest and the town of uncertain name lay beside them straddling a creek that presumably took its head somewhere in the . . . things . . . and traveled south and east from there.

The town consisted of a smattering of wood-frame stores and small houses, only a very few of which were constructed of logs or hewn timbers. Apparently someone had set up a sawmill early in the town's history because nearly all the buildings in sight were made of milled lumber.

For the past several days the country they'd passed through was mostly grassland with little timber growing on it and that mostly cedar. The slopes of the whatever-they-were above Ki'iwa were forested, which no doubt explained the sawmill and lumber operations. Dex suspected that a man with lumber to sell in this mostly barren country would be in much the same position as the fellow who held the keys to the mint.

"What d'you think?" he asked.

"I think I don't much care what they call this place. My ass hurts. I'd like to stop here," James said.

"All right, but I think I'd best go by a fake name. Just in case those posters have found their way this far."

James grinned. "How 'bout Lewis?" It was the name of Dexter's very slightly younger twin brother. Neither was fond of the other. And that was an understatement of considerable proportion.

"How about you shove it up your black ass?"

James's grin grew wider. "If that's what you want to call yourself, listen, it's okay by me. I can just call you 'ass' for short."

"I'll think of something," Dex said as he kneed his horse into a slow walk to cover the remaining quarter mile or so into Ki'iwa in the Indian Territories. Or Texas. Whichever.

· 4 ·

"My name is John Milton, and I'll be needing a room if you please."

"Yes, sir. One room for the both of you gentlemen?" the desk clerk asked without batting an eye.

Dex, however, blinked.

This was . . . most unusual. Most hotels in his experience would have called the law out, or perhaps a group of men with clubs and hard-kicking boots, before they would admit a black man. Dex and James generally used the subterfuge that James was Dexter's manservant and had a cot brought in or a pallet thrown onto the floor lest a Negro soil the sheets of an honest inn.

Here . . .

Dex took another look at the clerk. The fellow seemed ordinary enough. Dark hair. Tanned complexion. Business suit with a tie and reasonably fresh starched batwing collar. Then he turned to fetch a key down from the rack behind the counter and Dex saw a long, gleaming black braid hanging down his back.

An Indian, by damn.

"Have we crossed into the Nations?" he asked.

"Oh, yes. Ten, twelve miles back if you're coming up

from Texas," the man said as he turned back to the counter and dropped a pair of heavy keys on it. "Twenty-five cents a night apiece, gents. There's fresh linen on the beds and the price includes one towel for each. No charge for a pitcher of hot water, but if you want a tub and water for that it'll be an extra dime. And we'd appreciate it if you'd take your boots off before you go to bed."

"We'll try to keep that in mind," James said.

The clerk smiled. "I don't mean to be insulting, sir. You might be surprised how many gentlemen don't think of it without we remind them."

"Sorry," James mumbled.

"I take it you gents are new to the Territory?" the clerk asked.

Dex nodded.

"You may or may not know then that federal law prohibits the sale of alcoholic spirits to an Indian. Not many places around here bother to sell liquor, but some do. If anyone asks you to buy a drink for them, I'd recommend that you decline. Politely, but decline. It would save trouble for everyone. Including quite a lot of it for you if you're caught. And you never know who will turn out to be a federal officer." He smiled. "Perhaps even you for all any of us knows."

"Thank you for the instruction," Dex said.

"Now if you would both sign the register, please." The clerk—the man wasn't nearly as dark as Dex had been led to believe Indians would be; but then what the hell did he know? he'd never actually encountered one before this moment, at least not to his own knowledge—produced a pen and ink bottle and set them next to a canvas-bound ledger book.

Theirs were the only names entered for the past four days, Dex saw. He signed. As John Milton. James did too. As James Emory. Dex knew where that came from. Dex, and therefore James by association, once attended Emory College in Oxford, Georgia. Good school.

"Would you like us to pay in advance?"

"If it would be convenient, sir."

Dex nodded and gave him two dollars. The clerk lifted an eyebrow.

"We expect to be here several days," Dex explained. "If you have room for us, that is."

"I believe we can accommodate you, gentlemen," the Indian clerk said with a perfectly straight face. He made no mention of the little hotel being otherwise unoccupied.

"Thanks."

Dex was halfway up the single flight of steps to the second floor when it occurred to him that he had no earthly idea what last name James normally went by.

They'd been best friends since they were infants, and for no reason whatsoever it just wasn't something Dex ever thought about before this moment. James was just . . . James. But he had to have a last name. His mother . . . his mother may well *not* have had a last name to pass along to him, as a matter of fact. She'd been a slave most of her life, owned by Dexter's father Charles Yancey and then employed as the family cook until she was given a house and plot of land to retire onto late in life.

But a name? If she had one, Dex never heard it. If James had one . . .

Dex was not sure if he wanted to talk about this or not. He was damned well embarrassed to bring it up, for one thing. How does one go about asking one's lifelong best friend what his *name* is? Jesus! Dex thought. Not knowing it, not ever thinking about it . . . it was unconscionable. It was also true.

He plodded on up the stairs and turned right into the hallway, checking the number on a tag that dangled from the big key and searching for a matching door number.

• 5 •

"John Milton, eh?"

Dex smiled and shrugged.

"If you think it was paradise that we put behind us, lost or otherwise . . ."

Dex's smile turned into a laugh. "Not hardly." Neither their last weeks back home—well, what used to be home but was no longer—in Louisiana nor their more recent experiences in Texas could have been considered anything worthy of paradise. "But I've been thinking about the poetry. And the thoughts behind it."

"When you get to thinking about poetry, white boy, it usually means there's a pretty girl in the neighborhood. Is there something you haven't been telling me about why we wound up here in . . . whatever this place is properly called?"

"Hell, there probably is a girl around here pretty enough that I'd want to impress her with some poetry. I just haven't met her yet."

"Good. I'm glad we got that out of the way. Now which bed do you want?"

The hotel room was rather nice, everything considered. There were two beds, narrow but with real springs under the mattresses. Two thick blankets on each bed and, as promised, spanking fresh linen. A window—Dex walked over to it and checked—overlooked the main street of Ki(something)iwa. There was no wardrobe but pegs were provided for hanging clothing, and there was a small chest of drawers for those who wanted to unpack and make themselves comfortable. A side table held a basin and pitcher of water, and there were lamps on nightstands beside the head of each bed. The management had even been thoughtful enough to provide boxes of sulphur-tipped matches, and the lamps were clean and heavy with oil. Dex sniffed. Whale oil, the real thing and not the cheaper but less pleasantly scented coal oil.

"Not bad," he said.

"You didn't say which bed you want."

"Whichever one you don't," Dex said agreeably.

"I tell you, I could get used to this idea of being treated like a real person. Allowed to sleep in a proper bed and everything." James whistled. "Makes me feel damn near white." Then he grinned. "D'you have any idea how bad that *worries* me?" He dropped his saddlebags onto the bed nearer the window.

Dex took the other bed and began unpacking.

"You want to stay here awhile?" James asked.

"Why not. It seems a nice enough place, and you'll feel better if you can stay out of the saddle for a spell. We have money enough to get along for a while and nowhere we have to get to in any big hurry. Yeah, I think it'd be a good idea to stay here for . . . I dunno . . . a week or two. Rest up some and move on whenever we damn well feel like it."

"That sure sounds good to me." James stretched out on the bed with an exaggerated sigh and laced his hands behind his neck.

"Weren't you paying attention? Take your boots off."

James shifted his feet to the side so his boots were hanging off the edge of the bed.

◆ 6 ◆

"Where the hell are you going?" Dex demanded as James continued moving along the board sidewalk. Dex had stopped outside the cafe the hotel clerk pointed them toward. James did not.

"Around back of course."

"I don't think you have to do that."

James gave him a look of mild impatience. "Dexter, how old am I? Twenty-seven, in case you've forgotten. Do you know how many times I've gone into a restaurant with you and sat at the same table to eat a meal or drink a drink? Do you?"

"Near as I can figure it," Dex answered, "the figure would be somewhere in the neighborhood of none."

"Exactly," James returned. "Never. Not once. For damn good reason. And if it's all the same to you, I'd just as soon not get myself beat up again today. I haven't finished healing from the last time, and I don't want to put any bumps on top of my bruises. Okay?"

"I don't think they feel that same way around here," Dex said. "You saw how that Indian back at the hotel treated you. You're as welcome as anybody else."

"And I liked it, true enough. But how do we know it'd be the same in this place?"

Dex shrugged. "How do we know it wouldn't? I tell you what, James. We'll both go in and if anybody says anything I'll tell them of course I had no intention of letting you sit there with the white folks to eat. Then I'll cuss you some . . . tell you to mind how you act . . . and send your black ass into the kitchen to eat on the back stoop or something."

James looked doubtful. But after a moment's reflection he nodded.

Inside the cafe no one batted an eye at the presence of a black man and a white together. They took seats, ordered, ate an adequate if not exactly outstanding meal together and none of the other customers paid any particular attention to either one of them.

Later James seemed damn near overwhelmed by the experience, although to Dex it hadn't been anything all that unnerving.

"I can't . . . God, Dex. You don't know how that felt."

"No," Dex said softly, "I guess I really don't. All these years we've been together and I hadn't really thought about a little thing like that. Not from your point of view, I hadn't."

"Little? Jesus, Dex, you call it little? It's the damnedest thing that's ever happened to me. I wouldn't call it little."

Dex remembered anew the thoughts he'd had—the still unresolved thoughts—that he did not know what surname James used. If indeed he'd ever before had occasion to so identify himself.

"What do you say we push our luck while it's rolling," Dex suggested, "and go find a saloon."

James grinned. "You buying?"

"Damn right I am," Dex agreed.

"Then lead on. I'll be right behind you."

"Beside me might be better."

James's grin got bigger.

• 7 •

The bartender, a thin man with a wisp of limp mustache struggling to grow on his upper lip, served up a foamy beer—somewhat too much foam actually—to Dexter without hesitation, but he paused before he set the matching mug in front of James.

"You wouldn't happen to be Indian, would you?"

James scowled. "Do I look like an Indian to you?" he demanded.

"You're new in this town," the bartender returned. "Are you new in the Nations too?"

"I am. What of it?"

"Don't know many Seminoles, huh?"

"Mister, I don't even know what a Seminole is," James told him. Which Dex knew to be an exaggeration to put it politely, an out and out lie to be more accurate about it. The Seminoles were a tribe of Indians, as James knew every bit as well as Dex did. In school they'd read much about the several wars the Seminoles conducted with the United States. Four of them, if Dex remembered correctly. But the Seminole tribe was way the hell and gone down south in the swamps of Florida. This was the Indian Territory, not Florida. And there likely wasn't a proper swamp any closer to Ki(something)iwa than the bayous back home in Louisiana.

"You look like a Seminole to me," the bartender said.

"You're shitting me."

"I'm not," the barman insisted. "There's lots of black Seminoles. They took in plenty of runaway slaves, starting all the way back to when the British owned that country. Adopted them into the tribe. Married. Had kids, of course. Now you, you got thin lips and a regular nose. Could be you're part white, but there's plenty of Seminoles look just like you. And I'd have trouble with the law if I was to sell beer to a Seminole."

"I'm not a Seminole," James said, all traces of imminent belligerence gone from his voice.

"Thank you." The barkeep set the frothy mug onto the bar in front of James and collected a dime from Dex for the pair of drinks.

James looked rather pleased, Dex thought, although whether it was over being mistaken for an Indian or simply because he was welcome to have a drink here along with other folks Dexter wasn't sure.

As for himself, Dex wished the bartender didn't put such a head on the beer. It was tasty enough and a little foam is proof of freshness, but even good things can be taken to extremes.

He took another swallow, just to verify his first impression of the quality of the brew, then sidled a few feet to his right to where a free lunch spread was laid out on a tray woven from willow withes.

He was joined there by another man who stood unnecessarily close, so close that their elbows jostled together.

Dex expected an apology. Instead the man leaned even nearer and in a low, hoarse whisper said, "The man's been waiting for you. Go out back like you need to take a crap. Somebody will meet you behind the outhouse an' guide you from there. Midnight. Sharp. Don't be late."

Dex felt a weight in his right hand coat pocket. Before he could protest or so much as feel to see what had been slipped into his pocket, the man turned and walked away in a lanky but deceptively swift stride.

Dex turned to James. "Have you ever seen that guy before?"

James merely looked puzzled. "What guy?"

"You didn't see him?"

"See who?"

Unfortunately Dex had no answer to give.

· 8 ·

No wonder he'd noticed the weight when it entered his pocket. The object the man had put there was a small leather pouch. It proved to be a coin purse. It also proved to hold three hundred dollars in shiny new double eagles. Fifteen of them and each one as pretty as Lady Liberty herself, she whose image graced them wrought of gold.

James whistled when he saw what Dex had. They were standing in the mouth of an alley adjacent to the saloon. Dex's curiosity had been too great for him to wait until they got all the way back to the hotel. And the manner of delivery was such that he hadn't even considered looking into the pocket while they were still indoors where others might see.

"What the hell is this about?" James asked.

The only answer Dex had was a shrug. An eloquent shrug perhaps but a shrug of dismay nonetheless. He explained what had happened back there.

"The man is waiting? What man?"

Dex could only shrug again. Then he added, "The rich man, I'd say."

"So rich he gives money away to strangers?"

The customary shrug followed that suggestion too.

"And you're to meet him at midnight, huh. Will you?"

Dex grinned. "Three hundred dollars delivered now implies there should be more to come later, wouldn't you think? Yeah, I'll go see this guy. If nothing else I'll give him his money back and tell him he made a mistake. We have enough trouble with Jane Carter and her posters. We don't want some stranger thinking we've robbed him and coming after us too."

"I don't suppose you'd consider . . . no, never mind. I don't feel up to making another run for the border right now." James smiled too. "Besides, the only border close enough to run to would put us right back into Texas, and I sure don't want that again. An' the next damn border up the ladder is pretty far away."

"You could always find out where these Seminoles live and pass yourself off as one," Dex suggested.

"And what about you, white boy? You don't look much like an Indian."

"Nah. Wouldn't want to give up drinking anyhow. I'll just say I'm your faithful servant John Milton."

"Gee, am I a rich Indian?"

"Between what we have in your money belt and this three hundred, you're close enough to it for now." Their habit was for James to carry their money hidden on his person on the theory that would-be robbers were unlikely to suspect a black servant of having anything on him worth stealing. Dex carried only enough in his own pockets to meet their daily needs.

"You want me to tuck that three hundred away?"

Dex shook his head. "I expect I'll be giving it back in a few more hours. What I do want you to do is go back to the hotel and change into dark clothes. Get out of that white shirt in particular."

"Somehow I get the idea that you want me to be lurking in the shadows when you meet this guy," James said.

"It's a role you were born to play," Dex told him.

James glanced down at his own chocolate-colored flesh and grinned. "Ain't nobody gonna spot this po' ol' dinge, bawss. I'se be jus' one mo' shadow on de groun'."

"Did something happen to your mouth? That beer pucker you up or something? You're talking funny."

James laughed. "You go back inside if you like. Just be careful you don't get drunk. Or lose track of time. The man doesn't want you to be late. And don't worry about me. You won't see me, white boy, but I'll be there."

"And your revolvers," Dex reminded. "Just in case."

"Gosh, I'm glad you reminded me of that. I might've forgot."

"Sarcasm is unbecoming."

"Yowzuh, massa suh, yowzuh."

Dex laughed and clapped his old friend on the shoulder. James would be there when the time came, he knew, and if help was needed James and his pistols would provide it. Dex knew he could count on that if on nothing else.

"I'll see you later. Or rather . . . I won't see you." Dex dropped the very pleasantly heavy little poke back into his pocket and returned to the saloon while James headed up the street in the direction of the hotel.

◆ 9 ◆

The ground felt spongy underfoot and the stench was damn near overwhelming. Dex figured whoever dug the hole for this back-alley shitter was getting paid by the job and not the hour because he sure must have done a half-assed job of it. Uh, so to speak. Either that or the two-holer was so popular it was almost full, because it really felt like the ground would give way and drop him into the aromatic brown soup if he got any closer to the back wall of the outhouse. He moved a couple steps away to where there wasn't so much give under his shoes and felt considerably the better for it. It still smelled worse than a pigsty in summer, but at least he wasn't in danger of falling neck deep into other peoples' shit.

"Leaving so soon?"

The sound of a voice coming out of nowhere startled the hell out of him. Dex jerked his head around in the direction the words came from, but he saw nothing there except shadows. "Where are you?"

By the way of an answer the shape of a man materialized out of the side of a head-high weed. It was too dark for Dex to see anything beyond the simple fact that someone was standing there, though. "Are you the man I'm supposed to meet here?"

"No, but I'm the man that will take you to the man you're supposed to meet tonight."

"I didn't bring a horse," Dex said, hoping James was lurking close enough to overhear just in case the answer was such that James should slip away and get his horse too.

"You won't need one," the dark figure told him.

"All right."

"Go down to the mouth of the alley. No, that way, not back there. Go to the street and turn right. When you get to the next corner, stop. Wait there."

"Will this . . . will 'the man' be there?" Dex asked.

There was no answer. The figure stepped backward and was instantly invisible again even though by this time Dex had had more than enough time for his eyes to adjust after the lamplight inside the saloon.

Dex shrugged—the gesture seemed to be becoming a habit this evening although with mighty good reason—and followed the alley in the direction the shadowy fellow indicated.

He reached the street without any more incident than startling the hell out of a stray cat—which seemed entirely fair since the damned cat startled the hell out of Dex too when it hissed and took off running—and turned to his right. Walked to the corner and stopped.

And stood there. And waited. And stood there.

A man and woman—she was much too pretty and smelled too nice to've been the man's wife—passed by.

A trio of drunks wandered past.

Dex continued to stand where he was.

He might have decided this was a prank of the sort enjoyed by initiates into Greek societies except for the three hundred dollars that still weighed heavy in his right-hand coat pocket. Three hundred dollars made the mystery serious indeed.

But he still didn't like having to stand there and wait half the damned night away.

Eventually he was joined on the corner by the same fel-

low who'd been in the saloon early in the evening, the same
one who'd dropped the purse into his pocket.

"Come with me."

Dex frowned. He'd heard the man whisper to him before.
And then he'd heard a normal speaking voice back beside
the outhouse. Both had come from this same man.

"What the hell'd you keep me waiting here for?"

"I had to make sure you weren't being followed, didn't
I?"

Dex grunted. Obviously James saw what the fellow was
up to, staying in the shadows back there like that, and out-
waited him. Dex still didn't like standing on a street corner
in the middle of the night like that, but at least now he
knew there'd been a good reason for it. "You'll take me to
the man now?"

"Just hold your questions and follow me, okay?" The
man turned and set out at a brisk clip toward the east edge
of Ki(something)iwa.

Dex shut his mouth and followed.

· 10 ·

Three bridges crossed the creek that seemed to have given Ki(something)iwa its existence. One, situated more or less in the center of town, was a substantial affair capable of carrying heavy wagon traffic. The others, one upstream from the town center and the other down were little more than oversized footbridges. They might support a donkey cart or light buggy but nothing heavier than that.

The man Dex was following detoured into the residential outskirts of the town and approached the downstream bridge. When he reached it, however, he turned aside, taking a narrow footpath that led to the creek bank and the thick growth of trees and dense brush that lined the waterway.

Dex stumbled and muttered as they entered a copse of— he thought—live oak. There was little enough moonlight out on the road. Beneath the trees it was dark as a lawyer's soul.

"Slow down," Dex said.

"Shhh," was the only answer he received. But the man slowed down.

They continued along the south side of the creek for a quarter mile or so. Dex could not see beyond the screen of

brush they were walking through, but he was fairly sure
the last houses would have been left behind by now. He
tripped, muttered unhappily and was thinking about telling
his guide to slow down even more when without warning
they emerged onto a point created by a bend in the stream.

There were still trees, although fewer here, but the thick
undergrowth had been cleared, probably by natural forces
during spring flooding. The effect was parklike and pretty.
It also allowed moonlight to penetrate the grassy flat so that
Dex could see a carriage standing in the shelter of an ancient, massive oak tree.

"He's waiting for you inside," the guide said. "Just go
ahead and get in." The man made no effort to approach the
carriage himself but motioned Dex forward.

"What about you?"

"I'll be here making sure nobody sneaks up close enough
to listen."

"I see." That was all right by Dex, actually. He didn't
need for James to overhear. What he wanted James to do
was protect his backside. Dex could do whatever listening
was necessary for the both of them.

Dex cleared his throat as he approached the side of the
carriage, mostly to announce his presence to whoever was
waiting inside. With all this secrecy it seemed entirely possible to him that "the man" might be a mite spooky. And
getting shot in the middle of the night—or any other time—
could mess up an otherwise interesting evening.

"Come." The voice was deep and gravelly.

Dex opened the carriage door and had to search with his
foot for a moment to locate the steel step bolted under the
wagon frame. He pulled himself into the covered rig.

"Close the door."

Dex did so.

"Is the side curtain down?"

He checked it by feel. The inside of a grave couldn't
have been any darker. "It's down."

"Good."

He heard the scrape of a match and instantly there was
a flare of yellow flame. The match flame was bright enough

after so much darkness that it hurt his eyes and for a moment he squinted against the glare.

The man touched the match to the wick of an opera lamp attached to the back wall of the carriage and then used the same match to light another lamp on the opposite side.

Dex blinked. Not from the light this time but with a mild degree of surprise.

The man could have qualified as several men. Hell, he could've counted as three normal-sized adult males. If the count was based, that is, on bulk and poundage.

The man occupied the backseat of the carriage.

The man occupied *all* of the backseat of the carriage.

Dex didn't think—no, that wasn't correct; Dex was purely positive—he'd never seen any one human person that big before. Or anyway that fat. There was no way for him to judge how tall the man would have been had he been standing erect. If, that is, he was capable of supporting himself on the tree-stump appendages that were his legs. For all Dex knew he might be a short, squat little fucker. But there wasn't any doubt whatsoever that he was a wide one. With this man on board, the carriage would've had to take the middle bridge if it were to cross the creek. His weight would surely have collapsed either of the two lesser bridges . . . even if he was afoot when he crossed.

He had more chins than Dex bothered to count. Eyes that looked like tiny black raisins set into suet although on closer inspection Dex realized there was nothing unusual about the eyes themselves. It was simply that they were dwarfed by the mass that surrounded them.

His nose was a lump in the middle of that suet pudding, his mouth a thin and nearly lipless slash.

Yet huge and misshapen though he was, the man was immaculately groomed and tailored. Every hair on his head was carefully trimmed. His cheeks were pink and closely shaved even at this miserable time of night, and he smelled of bay rum and talcum powder.

He wore a dark suit with matching vest, a perfectly knotted tie and displayed a watch fob from one vest pocket that had a gold nugget dangling from it large enough to provide for the needs of a family of six for a year and a half.

The watch chain attached to that fob and draping across several feet of belly to reach the watch pocket, Dex thought, could have served double duty as an anchor chain on a fair-sized boat. It too was of gold.

The man Dex observed, was not impoverished.

"You were supposed to be here last week," the man said by way of greeting.

Dex merely shrugged. He got the impression that this wealthy soul would like for others to defer to him, and Dex was damned if he would do that. There was just something about the gross and overbearing fellow—not his appearance exactly but his attitude—that Dex found to be grating. He refused to offer an apology . . . especially since there was quite obviously a wee small mix-up as to the matter of identities.

On the other hand, Dex didn't especially want to give any explanations either. Not, at least, right now. After all, three hundred dollars in hand and an implied promise that more would follow . . . that was certainly enough to pique a boy's interest.

Dex kept his expression neutral, therefore, and his mouth closed. He would listen to whatever the man wanted to say before he decided what to do about it. If anything.

· 11 ·

"Are you clear on what I require of you?" the man asked.

"No, I am not," Dex told him.

"Berdecker explained it all to you, didn't he? Enough of it, anyway?"

Dex had never met nor heard of anybody named Berdecker. And the fellow couldn't be the one who'd guided him here or there would not have been any confusion about Dex's identity. "Anything that a man hears secondhand is subject to error," he said. "I want to hear it straight from you. All of it."

Under other circumstances Dex might have used the phrase "straight from the horse's mouth." Not this time. This guy was heftier than some horses and might well have taken that for a deliberate taunt. Probably not a good idea.

The man looked mildly annoyed.

Dex reached into his pocket, withdrew the pouch of gold coins and handed them to the man, whose eyebrows shot toward the ceiling even as he quite automatically reached out to accept what was being handed to him.

"We can forget the whole thing," Dex suggested, "and part company with no hard feelings." He touched the brim of his hat in silent salute and reached for the door handle.

"No!" the fat man said quickly.

Dex paused. But he did not pull his hand back, instead allowing it to remain poised with his fingers tight on the handle.

"You're a touchy one, aren't you?" the man complained.

"I prefer to think of myself as being independent."

The man reached inside his coat, and for a moment Dex considered flinging himself out into the covering protection of the night. But all the man brought into view was a handkerchief. He took his time unfolding it and using it to mop his cheeks, forehead and neck. It was not particularly warm inside the carriage despite the lack of air circulation, but the fat man was perspiring rather heavily. He wiped himself—Dex thought the time required to do that deliberately extended so as to give himself time to think, perhaps deciding how much to disclose and how much to withhold—then refolded the handkerchief with meticulous care and returned it to his pocket before he spoke again.

"What I want is not . . . not a simple job of killing. You should understand that. If all I wanted was a murder I could have found a dozen men cheaper and frankly easier to get along with. What I need you to do is to arrange an accident. Or what will pass as one. Is that what you wanted to hear? You wanted to hear me say it, right straight from the horse's mouth?"

Okay, so the guy wasn't all that sensitive to comments about size.

Wasn't all that delicate either when it came to what he would ask of his hired help.

"What I want to hear from you," Dex said calmly, "is every detail of your requirements. Anything I hear before is worthless. I will act . . . or won't, depending on whether I agree to take this job or not . . . only on what I hear from your own mouth."

The fat man frowned. Again went through the ritual with the folded handkerchief.

And began once more to speak.

◆ 12 ◆

"You come highly recommended, Chance," the fat man said.

Chance. Dex gathered that was the name of the person the man expected to see here. No idea if Chance was the first name or last, but this was a start.

"I registered at the hotel under the name John Milton," Dex said. "It's a good name. Why don't we stick with it, if you don't mind."

"You are an educated man, Mister . . . Milton?"

"I've read a little, if that's what you're asking."

"I suppose it shouldn't make any difference, but somehow that makes me feel better about choosing you."

"What would you like me to call you?" Dex asked. He had no idea if he was supposed to already possess that information courtesy of the never-met Mr. Berdecker.

"Everyone here knows my real name. And you'll have no need to mention me to anyone anyway," the fat man informed him. "After tonight you and I shall not meet again. I assume you have sense enough to refrain from discussing me or anything about me." He permitted himself a thin smile that held no hint of humor in it. "And I am confident you'll not be talking to anyone else about the, shall we say, the *work* you will be undertaking for me."

Dex grunted. "Tell me more about this work, pray."

"What a truly odd choice of wording. One doesn't think of prayer in conjunction with . . . you know."

"Murder," Dex supplied for him. He smiled. "But made to seem an accident."

The fat man cleared his throat and managed to look just the least bit embarrassed.

"I interrupted you. Sorry. Do go on, please."

"The, um, target of your attentions . . ."

"That's a very nice way to put it," Dex injected.

"Thank you. As I was saying, the target of your attentions will be Wilhelmina Stout. I know Berdecker already informed you that the person is, um, of the female persuasion."

"Yes," Dex agreed in an easy lie.

The fat man shook his head. "I doubt you have any idea how very few, uh, businessmen of your, um, chosen profession . . . so few will accept assignments involving women, don't you see."

"You say that as if I should apologize."

"No. Please. Don't misunderstand me. I was merely struck by the, uh, incongruity."

"I can see how you might be. Priests and preachers, it's the same with them too," Dex said pleasantly, sort of getting into the feel of this silliness now and beginning to make stories up as he went along. He shook his head and managed a mournful expression. "There are so few standards these days. So little pride in workmanship. I don't mind telling you, there are moments when I wonder about the integrity of my, um, peers."

The fat man looked startled. Good. Dex intended him to be.

"We're digressing," Dex said. "Please get back to the particulars of your requirements."

"Yes, well, the exact specifics will be up to you, of course. I only require that Miss Stout experience her unfortunate accident no later than the thirtieth day of next month."

"That should give me ample time," Dex said. "Am I correct in understanding that a date sooner than that would also be acceptable."

"Oh, yes. Entirely acceptable, thank you."

"And the method will be at my discretion," Dex said.

"Yes, quite so."

Dex nodded. "Now as to my fees . . ." He let the question hang not quite asked in the rather close air between them. Damned if the fat man wasn't taking up most of that too, not only room but the very air. He was sweating heavily now, and Dex could feel perspiration begin to bead on his forehead as well.

"I am sure Berdecker told you that your customary fee is entirely acceptable to me. The amount already paid is a non-refundable fee for travel and other expenses." With a grimace and a loud groan the fat man bestirred his great bulk to turn sideways and lean precariously down to reach something on the floor of the carriage. Dex hoped the big son of a bitch didn't lose control of all that weight and topple over. He was sure to bust something if he did. The frame of the carriage came first to mind.

The fat man produced a very small leather valise and handed it to Dexter, along with the pouch Dex had returned to him earlier. "The first half of your fee," he said. "Precisely as agreed upon."

"Thank you." Dex accepted the bag and dropped it casually onto the seat at his side. Something inside it was for damn sure heavy.

The fat man cleared his throat and ran a finger beneath the collar of his shirt. The collar had been fresh at the start of this conversation but was beginning to wilt now. It really needed to be replaced.

"I want, uh, I want you to know that if the, um, if the date is met and no suspicions are attached to the lady's demise . . . let me stress that . . . if there are no suspicions at all, I will add a rather substantial bonus to your fee, Mr. Drewery."

Chance Drewery. Sounded to Dex like a made-up name. But then a fellow wouldn't likely want the folks back home hearing about his fame in this particular field of endeavor, would he?

And what the hell. It was certainly as good a made-up name as John Milton was. Or James Emory. Dex was hardly in a position to criticize on that account.

"You did say 'substantial,' did you not, sir?" Dex asked in a chipper and eager tone.

"Half again," the fat man confirmed, "over and above your normal fee."

"It's a pleasure doing business with you, sir." Dex smiled and offered his hand. The man's handshake felt like Dex was gripping lukewarm sausages. But the valise felt just fine in his other hand.

"I trust we'll not be seeing each other again, Mr. Drewery. Good luck."

"And to you, sir." Dex smiled again, touched the brim of his hat and reached for the door handle.

"One moment, please."

Dex paused, and the fat man extinguished first one lamp and then the other. Only when the carriage was totally dark again did he say, "Good night, Chance."

"Good night."

There was no sign of the guide now. Dex stayed where he was for a few seconds to let his eyes adjust to the darkness. Although in truth it was much less dark now than when he'd come. He thought he could already detect a faint paling in the eastern sky.

No sign of the guide, Dex saw, nor any of James either.

Still, he didn't want to stand there lollygagging lest someone wonder why he kept peering about.

He took a fresh grip on the valise, glanced quickly around one last time and began the walk back to Ki(something)iwa.

· 13 ·

Dex looked at the stacks of bright, beautiful, gleaming golden coins and whistled softly under his breath.

One thousand five hundred dollars. In coin. Every coin looking brand-new and mint-fresh.

Damn but the double eagle was a handsome thing. Dex liked them. Quite a lot.

And a pile of them this large was . . . impressive.

Oh, he'd seen more money than this at one time. Of course he had. But on those occasions before he'd observed an assortment of rumpled currency and coins in many denominations.

There was something particularly captivating about this collection of unsullied gold, each piece new and unworn, each disc of precious metal perfect as to color, shine and impressed design.

One thousand five hundred dollars in hand now. That meant Chance Drewery's fee totalled three thousand. Plus expenses. Of course expenses would be additional. Why the hell not. And a bonus if Wilhelmina Stout died an unquestionably accidental death on or before the thirtieth day of next month.

Dex frowned in thought. This was . . . he wasn't sure.

The nineteenth. Twentieth. Somewhere around then. In any event he had more than a month in which to resolve this rather thorny little problem.

Thorny in that he had absolutely no intention of murdering an innocent woman. Or, hell, murdering any woman, innocent or not.

Yet at the same time, he had no intention of returning this rather charming pile of glittering wherewithal.

Wherewithal for what? Why, for whatever.

For life. For joy. For the pleasures of wonderfully riotous living. For ancient brandy and for women so fancy they'd make peacocks blush with shame. For the finest vintages of wine. For champagne and oysters. For evenings at the orchestra. The opera. The ballet.

Not that any such were likely to be found close by. But they should have civilized pursuits in Kansas City, say. Or in Colorado Springs, which the social arbiters were already referring to as Newport in the Rockies.

Dex had never been to either city. He saw no reason now why he should not visit—and thoroughly enjoy—both.

Well, no reason except perhaps one very small one.

James was in no condition to be making a run for Kansas. Not with Jane Carter and surely the fat man both in a lather of pursuit as surely would happen if they were to pocket the money, eighteen hundred of it counting the advance against expenses, and amble off without the courtesy of earning their pay.

A person of the fat man's inclinations and wallet would no doubt be an even more determined foe than the lovely Miss Carter.

No, dammit, Dex did *not* want *two* wealthy and vindictive enemies lusting to see his head on a platter.

But, dammit all, he didn't want to give the man back his money either.

Besides, it seemed a trifle late to pop up with a shrug and an explanation that, sorry, he really wasn't Chance Drewery and he really wasn't in the business of killing folks.

No, he would just have to think of . . . something.

He had no idea what.

Talking with James would likely help, two heads being considerably better than one in the weightier matters.

And thinking of which, Dex rose from the side of the hotel room bed where he'd been perched while he basked in the beauty of all those lovely gold coins. He walked over to the window and peered out.

It was long past dawn now, well into full daylight. From the hotel room he could not see the sun, but nearly the entire east facing slope of the mountain wall to the west of Ki(something)iwa was receiving direct sunlight by now. Only a thin line of shadow stretched along the base of the mountain at this point. In another half hour at the most, Dex judged, the entire mountain chain would be lighted.

That long since Dex left the fat man in his carriage, and there was still no sign of James.

Dex began to worry.

If the guard-guide lurking in the trees had spotted James . . . no, surely Dex would have heard some sort of commotion if that happened. Wouldn't he?

He forced back a sudden impulse to leave the hotel and run back down along the little river so as to search the underbrush close to the glade where the carriage had been, just in case James had been waylaid and was lying there now injured and needing help.

Patience, Dex chided himself. He should have some patience. And some faith in James too.

But the waiting wasn't easy, damn it, now that he'd begun to worry.

All of a sudden the gold seemed no longer so pretty to him, no longer so worthy of admiration. Not, he realized, in comparison to the life and well-being of a friend.

· 14 ·

"Where the hell have you been?"

"Where the hell did you get all that money?"

"I asked you first," Dex snapped.

"Yeah, but what you have is a lot more interesting than what I've got."

"I've been worried about you," Dex complained.

"Aw, c'mon. There are times when it pays to be a spook. This is one of them."

"In broad daylight?"

James grinned. "Yeah, that was kinda the hard part."

"It's almost noon, damn you."

"You really were worried, weren't you?"

"I said that, didn't I?"

"I'm touched."

"You're going to be worse than touched if you do this again. Jeez, I send you to do one little thing and you take off like a hound after a coon."

"Except this time it's the coon doing the chasing," James said, his grin undiminished.

"Did you really have to do that?"

"Of course I did." James tossed his hat onto his bed and let his fingers riffle through the coins, knocking Dex's tidy stacks askew and quite obviously enjoying the sensation of feeling all that hard money.

"All of this, huh?"

"And it's only half our fee," Dex said.

James's eyebrows climbed halfway up his forehead. "How many people do we have to kill in order to earn that much money?"

"You might have meant that as a joke, but the answer is one. He wants us to kill a woman."

"You wanta tell me about it?" James forgot about the gold and went over to his bed. He sat down and began removing his shoes. They were damp, Dex saw, as were his socks.

Dex filled James in on everything the fat man said.

"Wilhelmina Stout," James repeated slowly when Dex was done. "With a name like that she must be one ugly old bag. Mr. Anderson's former wife, do you think, or maybe a business partner?"

"Who?" Dex asked.

"Anderson. You know."

"I don't know anybody named Anderson," Dex told him.

James gave him an odd look. "You just told me about meeting with him, didn't you?"

"His name is Anderson?"

"That's right. Leroy H. Anderson. I don't know what the H stands for but I suppose I could find out if you want me to."

"How the hell did you find out all this?"

The grin returned. "I had breakfast with his cook. She's a little old colored gal . . . well, maybe technically an Indian around here, but she's a pretty little ol' colored gal to me."

"How in hell . . . ?" Dex's voice was filled with wonder approaching downright awe.

"I followed the carriage back to Anderson's house, that's all. It wasn't far. His driver hung around in the weeds for a little while after you left, thinking to spot anybody that might have been following you, I suppose. Poor bastard wasn't very quiet about it though. He isn't near as good in the woods as I am, if I do brag on myself about it. I could've picked his pocket right there on the spot and he never would've known. Hell, clumsy as he is I maybe could've picked his nose for him too."

"Now there's a pretty thought."

"It's called simile, white boy. Look it up."

"I'll shove it up," Dex said. Then added, "Up your black ass."

"No way you could catch me. Anyhow . . . you want to hear about this Leroy Anderson fella or don't you?"

"I want to hear whatever you learned about him, yes thank you."

"Then hush and let me tell it. I drifted around in those woods quiet as morning fog until the driver, the one who met you out back of the saloon last night—his name is Carl, by the way—until this Carl fellow decided you hadn't been followed. It was almost daybreak by then. He left the brush and went over to the carriage. I was too far away to hear what he said, but he opened the door and spoke to Anderson for just a moment, then brought the horses up and hitched them."

"I never saw the horses."

"Two of them. They'd been staked out on the grass a little way downstream from where they left the carriage. I'd already found them and looked them over. Damn fine stock too. Not that Carl knows how to take proper care of a horse. The taller of the two has a gall on his left shoulder."

"Go ahead. About the people if you don't mind."

"I think I like the horses better than the people, but all right. After Carl got the team in harness, he drove west by south for about a mile. There's what I suppose you would call a ranch headquarters there. Fine looking big house. Not as fine as something you'd see back home in Louisiana, of course. It wouldn't be much as a plantation house. But for out in this sorry-ass country it looked pretty grand. Porches, fake columns, all that crap.

"There's a gate that the road leads through. No fence, mind you. Just the gate along with wings of three-rail white painted fence for about a hundred yards in each direction from the gate. It's all for show, of course, but it does make things look kind of pretty."

"Uh huh."

"There's the big house that I told you about. It has trees planted nice and orderly, but there isn't enough natural water in the soil. You can see where they've put little circle dams around the base of each tree to hold water. They must pump and carry it. Even so the trees aren't getting enough water. I don't know how long since they were planted, but I bet they won't last another year. They'll shrivel and die unless someone carries an awful lot more water to them than they're doing now.

"Let's see, there's the house and trees and a circular driveway that's been graveled and raked. And a bunch of outbuildings. Livestock pens. Like that. They're all made with milled lumber just like everything else around here."

"You still haven't told me about this breakfast with the pretty girl."

James smiled. "I hung around at a distance. Saw Carl help Anderson out of the carriage and inside. I could hardly believe the size of that man at first. Had to squeeze to get through the door of the carriage. And that was after Carl brought a set of steel steps down off the porch of the house for him.

"The guy eased down slow and careful, and once he was on the ground he had to use canes to walk with. There are steps at the front of the house leading up onto the porch, but Anderson didn't use them. Carl stopped the rig over to one side of the porch. There's like a shallow ramp there that Anderson can get up and down without having to use stairs. I bet his bedroom is downstairs too. The house is two stories tall, but I bet that man never sees the upstairs.

"Anyway, I waited until Anderson and his man Carl were inside. Then I walked right up the road in plain sight, whistling a lively air. Went around to the back of the house and rapped on the kitchen door. Jenny let me in."

"Jenny, is it now?"

James grinned.

"I told her I'm a traveling man and wondered could I

split her some wood off the pile in back in exchange for a bite to eat. She said there was plenty of help to chop the wood but that she'd be proud to fix me a meal. Fixed a good one too. Stick to the ribs stuff and all of it I could handle. She didn't object when I said after a meal like that I just might have to come back and ask for seconds."

"And I take it Jenny is a talkative little thing," Dex suggested.

"Isn't it nice that she is?" James said happily.

"Yes, it is. Because we're gonna have to figure out where we go from here. I'd like to find a way to keep this money."

"We could always shoot Wilhelmina Stout."

"Why, you dumb burrhead. We're supposed to make it look like an accident."

"Okay, so we ask this Miz Stout if she'd care to shoot herself but accidental like."

"Seriously, James. I'd like to find some way to work this thing to our advantage. Without, if you don't mind, committing mayhem on the person of the Stout woman."

"That do complicate matters, don't it?"

"It do," Dex conceded.

"I tell you what then. You think on it for a while. Me, I was up all night long creeping around in the bushes. I'll take a nap while you do the thinking for the both of us, white boy." He stretched out on the bed.

"Mind your shoes, dammit."

James chuckled. But he kicked his shoes off. He was asleep within seconds.

· 15 ·

"You know what I've been thinking?" Dex asked as he reached for a dinner roll. They were in the cafe again. It was the middle of the afternoon, and they were the only customers at the moment. The waiter, who Dex assumed was also the proprietor, had disappeared into the kitchen after serving them the late lunch both wanted after waking from their refreshing naps.

"Same as you're usually thinking. You're horny," James responded.

"Besides that."

"I didn't know you ever thought about anything besides pussy."

"I try not to but sometimes it sneaks up on me. Now can you be serious for a minute."

"If I have to. By the way, have I mentioned that Jenny is an awful lot better cook than whoever's back in the kitchen here?"

Dex ignored the diversion and said, "I've been wondering what's behind this thing between Anderson and Mrs. Stout. You know. Who they both are and why there's bad blood between them. I mean, it's especially curious that it isn't enough that the poor old thing be killed. It has to look like an accident."

"Insurance?" James guessed. "The lady could be insured against accidental death, and Anderson might be the beneficiary."

"That's a possibility, I suppose. To tell you the truth, though, I'd be more likely to think that if this were a big city. Out here in the middle of nowhere you wouldn't generally think in terms of insurance agents and stuff like that."

"Bull," James returned. "Insurance agents are like mice and fleas and other pests. They're every-damn-where."

"Yeah, but you'd think if these two were close enough for one to be the other's beneficiary on an insurance policy they'd at least have the same last name."

"Nah, there's a lot of reasons that could be. Business partners like we mentioned before. Or brother and sister. Anderson could be Miz Stout's maiden name."

"Possible," Dex conceded. Then he laughed. "I wonder."

"What?"

"What if Leroy Anderson and Wilhelmina Stout look alike?"

"God!" James rolled his eyes.

"I can just imagine the sight of somebody like him. But with tits. And wearing a dress."

James tried to hold his laughter back as he'd just finished taking a swallow of coffee. The effort failed. He broke up, spewing coffee out of his mouth and onto Dex and then spraying a fine mist of it through his nose.

Dex probably would have felt highly insulted. If he hadn't been laughing so hard himself.

The thought of a female version of Leroy Anderson was overwhelming to begin with. And James made it all the worse by gasping out the suggestion, "You could find out a lot from her if you were to snuggle up next to Miz Stout, Dexter. Solve your problem of being horny all the time too."

"Lordy, how would you get close enough to poke a hole buried that deep in fat?"

"You poor ol' short-pecker white boy. I feel sorry for

you if you have to ask a question like that. But don't you worry. Just slap a little bacon grease in whatever wrinkle is handiest and stick it in between the rolls." By way of illustration, James took up a dinner roll and squeezed the soft bread to form two rounded bulges with a crease between; then he slathered the top of the roll thick with butter and, rolling his eyes, proceeded to loudly mumble and snort while he licked the butter off again.

The thought behind James's teasing was simply too damned much for Dexter to cope with. He laughed until his stomach muscles ached and he was gasping for breath, then wheezed so loudly the waiter stuck his head out of the kitchen and asked, "Are you all right, mister?"

"I'm f . . . f . . . fine," Dex assured him after a small struggle to get the words out.

Which for some reason set James off again as he broke out in spasms of laughter mingled with coughing just as soon as the waiter retreated back into his kitchen.

· 16 ·

"Let me handle this," James said.

"If you think you can."

James gave Dex a dirty look and a roll of his eyes. "Subtlety is my strong suit, white boy."

"Fine. Show me," Dex told him.

They'd decided over lunch—once they were able to quit laughing and finish eating it—that the next logical step would be to find out just who and what this Wilhelmina Stout was.

"I'm kinda glad you want to do this," Dex said. "I never had aspirations to become a detective. A gigolo maybe but never a detective. How are you going to go about this investigation of yours?"

James merely grinned and led the way inside the hotel. "I've got a secret method. Watch me and learn," he whispered as instead of turning toward the staircase he veered in the direction of the unattended counter.

"Excuse me?" he called softly. And then, a little louder, "Is anyone here, please?"

The Indian desk clerk put in an appearance moments later. He had a spray of pale crumbs dribbling down the front of his vest and dropping onto the floor as he walked.

Cake? Dex speculated. Or cookies? Afternoon snack time in any event.

"Something I can do for you, sir?"

James propped an elbow onto the counter. "A fellow we met down south asked us to pay his respects to a woman who lives somewhere around here."

"Yes, sir?"

"We don't know the lady or where she lives. I was thinking perhaps you could help us. After all, we did promise this gentleman that we'd convey his compliments."

"And this lady would be . . . ?"

James told him. "Would you happen to know her?"

The clerk gave him a long but rather inscrutable look before he answered. "Everyone here knows the widow Stout, sir."

"Really."

"Of course, sir. Her late husband George Washington Stout founded this town."

"Oh my. I can see how everyone would know her, yes."

"I am surprised your friend in Texas did not mention that."

James grunted and said, "I am too now that I know. Oh well. Could be he assumed we'd already know. Not that it matters, I suppose."

"No, of course not," the Indian agreed.

"Would you mind telling us how we might find her, please," James persisted.

The clerk gave very simple instructions. "You go toward the mountains. The Stout place is the last house on that end of town. You can't miss it."

Dex's experience was that the statement "you can't miss it" was usually in error. But this hardly seemed worth picking a quarrel over.

"Thank you very much," James said. He glanced to his right, toward a clock on the wall.

"If you're thinking of visiting Mrs. Stout," the clerk offered, "you might want to do it now instead of waiting until morning. I, uh, I understand the lady prefers to sleep late.

She wouldn't welcome a call before noon, I think, and after two is even better."

"Thank you," James said. "Thank you very much. You've been a big help."

"My pleasure, sir."

James led the way back outside with a jaunty air. When they were on the sidewalk and well beyond the hearing of the hotel clerk he winked at Dex and said, "Did I tell you I could get the information, or what?"

"You also told me you had a secret method," Dex complained.

"Exactly," James said with considerable satisfaction. "And so I do." He grinned. "I ask."

Dex chuckled too as they walked briskly in the direction of the low line of hills which locally were thought to be mountains.

• 17 •

Damned if the Indian hadn't been right. They couldn't miss it. Or at the very least it would have been almighty difficult to miss.

The Stout house was a miniature version of a plantation manor house. It was set on a slight knoll with the mountains behind, the town below and the small river skipping noisily down a rock ladderway that was not high enough to be considered a waterfall but which was certainly more than one would want to tackle with a boat. White water in a boil of small rapids hissed and sprayed prettily.

The house was situated so that a covered verandah faced the rapids, and sets of swings suspended from the overhang would allow the Stouts and their guests to sit in the evenings looking at the swift-moving water and enjoying the bright and burbling sounds.

On the north side of the stream was the sprawl of a sawmill and attendant lumber stacks, outbuildings and the like. Natural timber, cut lumber and drying stacks were scattered about on that side of the river. A fourth bridge, this one a narrow footbridge with guardrails on both sides, crossed just above the rapids.

Judging from appearances, timber was cut somewhere on

the slopes of the mountains and the logs rafted downstream to the sawmill where they could be retrieved from the water and converted into usable material for building purposes.

Dex gathered that the late and presumably lamented George Washington Stout founded not only the town of Ki(something)iwa but also the sawmill that allowed it to be built here. Smart man, Dex guessed further. He managed to create a demand and then supply it in one simple maneuver. Tidy, that.

As for the house where the widow Stout was to be found, Dex had been in many that were more grand. But not lately. The house had been designed with loving attention to detail and would have fit quite nicely onto the grounds of nearly any plantation in Louisiana, Mississippi or Alabama—although he wasn't so sure about certain other parts of the South where folk were rumored to be uncultured and uncouth. It had multiple chimneys, multiple dormers, multiple roof peaks and multiple porches, all packed into and onto what was actually a fairly small structure.

"What d'you think?" James asked.

"I think I would have liked old Mr. Stout."

"Me too." James stopped.

"Something bothering you?" Dex asked.

"Nope. I kinda get the idea from looking at this place like you might do better inside there without me. I think you should go on alone from here."

"What will you be doing?"

James grinned. "I be goin' 'round back, bawss. See can this poor ol' boy beg him a bite t' eat, suh."

Dex grunted. "Good. That means I won't have to feed you later." He answered James's grin with one of his own and resumed his march toward the Stout residence.

"That ol' lady still could turn out to be Anderson's sister, y'know," James said softly from behind him. It was all Dex could do to keep himself from bursting into paroxysms of laughter once again.

· 18 ·

Damn that James anyway. He was free to chat up the house help while Dex would be stuck in the parlor talking to the widow Stout.

And the house help who'd just answered Dex's knock on the front door was toothsome indeed. In fact the girl looked downright edible to the point there probably should be a law against having carnal knowledge of her; something having to do with willful contamination of foodstuffs.

She was tall enough that she looked Dex pretty much eyeball to eyeball as she stood there in the open doorway, and she was slim. Dex liked slim. Nothing wasted, you see. It was obvious that she belonged to one of the Indian tribes as she had black hair so healthy it had a shiny gloss to it. She wore it loose, hanging straight and beautiful below her waist.

She had a narrow face, very large obsidian eyes, a wide mouth with exceptionally full lips—they looked invitingly soft too—and high, rather broad cheekbones. Her nose was prominent, large and hooked but narrow enough, a fact that somehow seemed to enhance rather than take away from her beauty.

Her skin was dark. Not the red or copper that Dex might

have expected but not black either. Brown, he decided after serious consideration; or dark olive. Damned attractive any-way.

If James got anywhere with this one he would be one lucky son of a bitch. Any man would be. And Dexter did not exclude himself from that assessment. He'd never had a black girl and would have felt odd doing so, sort of unfair and abusive, but there was nothing in his personal code of ethics and morality to prevent him from enjoying the charms of an Indian maiden. Or better yet, the charms of an Indian lass who was no longer a maiden.

This girl, he thought, would be a *very* pleasant introduc-tion to the idea of cross-cultural relationships.

This girl was damn-all pretty.

Just looking at her was enough to give him the begin-nings of a hard-on. Damned if he didn't hate the fact that he would have to ask after her mistress and let her go off to answer James's rap that soon would come at the back door of the Stout mansion.

"Is something wrong, sir? You're looking at me awfully strangely." Her voice was pure music, soft and throaty.

Dex tried to return his thoughts to the reason for his visit. But it wasn't easy. "Nothing's wrong. I, uh, need to speak with the widow Stout."

"About what?"

"I'm sorry. That would be confidential."

"Mrs. Stout does not accept just any jackanapes who calls, sir," the Indian girl informed him. "You'll have to do better than that."

Dex grinned. "It'll be fine with me if we have to stand here and discuss this for a while. I like the view fine as it is right now."

The girl laughed. She lowered her chin when she did so, covering her mouth and giggling behind her fingers.

She did not, however, close her eyes. And she could all too easily see the effect her appearance had on this stranger at the door. The front of Dex's trousers was bulging out-ward so hard the cloth flap at his fly spread apart and the buttons were on display. So too, albeit to a lesser extent, was the cause of this embarrassment.

Dex fully expected the door to be slammed in his face with a yelp and a squeal. Instead the girl began to laugh all the harder. "I must say, sir, I've had worse compliments."

She was, he concluded, no maiden then. Not particularly modest either. Hope welled in his breast. And in other places too.

The girl looked him in the eye again. This time her smile was less that which might be given to a casual stranger and more that of a young woman who was considering, say, a young man's invitation to dance.

"Could you be just a tiny bit specific about what you need to discuss with Mrs. Stout?"

Dex sighed. "I'm sorry. Really I am. But it wouldn't be fair to the lady for me to talk about this with anyone else. And it is most desperately important. I hesitate to utter this often overused, indeed ill-used phrase . . . but the truth is that my need to see her is quite genuinely a matter of life and death." He smiled. "Otherwise I assure you, I would rather hurry around to the back door so I could invent an excuse to come in and talk with you instead."

"It really is that important?"

"I'm afraid it is, yes."

She nibbled at her lower lip for a moment while she pondered the request. Then she took a step backward to vacate the doorway that she'd been blocking with her body. "I suppose you'd best come inside then."

"Thank you, miss." Dex carefully scraped his boots on a rag rug placed for that purpose outside the door, then stepped inside, hat in hand. The girl pointed to a set of deer antlers mounted atop a footed wooden post, and Dex hung his hat there.

It wasn't really fair. But he couldn't help himself. In a low voice he warned the girl, "You remember I told you I'd rather slip around back so I could talk to you in the kitchen? Well, my friend and partner is on his way to do just that. He'll be knocking at the kitchen door in another minute or two. I, uh, want you to know that he's not the only one interested." The grin flashed again. "And between the two of us, I'm much the better looking."

The girl seemed to get a kick out of that. She motioned for Dex to follow her, leading the way to a set of sliding double doors that she pulled back to reveal a large and handsomely furnished parlor. Before entering, however, she paused and in a loud voice called, "Pilar?"

"Yes'm." A moment later a plump, middle-aged woman with black hair done up in a severe bun appeared in the corridor that led past the staircase and into the back, presumably into the kitchen area.

"A gentleman will be calling at the back door in another few minutes' time, Pilar. Please show him in and bring him to the parlor when he does."

"Yes, ma'am," the woman said. She had a thick accent, but Dex hadn't enough experience to judge if she were Indian or perhaps Mexican.

The girl, he now realized although he hadn't given it any particular thought before, had unaccented English.

"Come this way, please."

Dex followed the strikingly lovely girl into the parlor.

· 19 ·

"You may sit there," the girl said, pointing to a rather severe and unupholstered cane bottom chair, one of a pair that flanked a small table in front of the room's side window.

Dex took the seat that was offered, and the girl settled herself into a large and very comfortable looking wingback armchair with a matching ottoman, both done in soft, pale leather.

"Oh, damn!" he blurted. "You're . . ."

The girl's look of smug delight was answer enough.

It hadn't occurred to him until that precise moment that *this* was the widow Wilhelmina Stout. "I'm sorry. I . . . never thought . . ."

She laughed. "It's all right. Really. George was almost exactly sixty years older than I. Obviously you didn't know that."

"Uh . . . no."

"And you would be . . . ?" she inquired in a soft voice.

Dex introduced himself. As Dexter Yancey. He wondered even as the name came off his tongue—but too late by just that much—if he should perhaps have told her John Milton instead. Or even Chance Drewery. After all, the fly-

ers Jane Carter sent around called for the head of Dexter
Yancey and not one of the alternates.

It was not easy, Dex was discovering, living under an
alias. Or several. A fellow had to remember too damn
much. It really was easier just being himself.

"And what may I ask, sir, is of such life-and-death importance that you must speak with me?"

"I, uh . . ." He was given a moment to reflect on how
much and how honestly he should explain by the appearance of Pilar at the door. The housemaid, as Dex realized
Pilar indeed actually was, had a rather confused looking
James in tow.

James had his hat in his hands and a look of interest in
his eyes. Particularly when he saw Wilhelmina Stout. But
then the girl was certain to have that effect on any red-
blooded male between the ages of, roughly, puberty and
three days after death.

Dex stood. "This is the friend and partner I was telling
you about. James, this lady is Wilhelmina Stout."

James blinked. Then shambled over to the other cane
bottom chair. Dex could tell that James wasn't quite sure
if he should go into his cornpone darky act or just be himself. He settled for keeping his mouth closed and his eyes
and ears open. Dex doubted that state would last very long,
but it was probably sensible enough for the time being.

The widow Stout, in the meantime, was giving them each
a close looking over, peering first at one and then the other.
"I see," she said at length. "You're brothers."

Dex looked at James, then smiled. "Almost," he said.
"We were raised as close as if we were." He did not go
into the details of former ownership or any of that.

Mrs. Stout shook her pretty head. "No, being close isn't
what I meant. You surely had the same father."

"We don't know who James's father was," Dex said automatically. Then he looked at James. "Do we?"

James too denied the relationship with a vigorous shake
of his head.

Mrs. Stout shrugged. "I'm sure you gentlemen have your
reasons for pretending otherwise, and I'll not question you

about them. But you can't fool me. Really. One look and I can see it plain as plain can be. Why you, Mr. Yancey," she was quite clearly addressing James when she spoke, which Dex found startling although not actually offensive, "would be the image of your twin if you only had his mustache and side whiskers. And you, Mr. Yancey," this time she spoke to Dex, "would be almost identical to your brother if your skin were dark." She peered at each of them again. "There is a difference of eye color too, of course. But if you want to see it for yourselves sometime, you should powder your face with cocoa sometime, Mr. . . . may I call you Dexter and James instead, please? It could become confusing if I try to distinguish between the two Messieurs Yancey otherwise."

"Well, um, sure. I suppose," Dex said.

James nodded his head. Well, Dex didn't blame him if James was feeling more than a little overwhelmed by all of this.

The widow Stout sat upright with a nod of satisfaction and a brisk clap of her hands. Obviously she'd settled that issue quite to her own satisfaction and was ready to move on to something else. "Now, gentlemen. What is it that you've come here to tell me?"

• 20 •

"We came here to kill you," Dex blurted. He hadn't known what was going to come out of his mouth until he heard the words himself. They were, he quite quickly conceded, a poor choice.

The girl stiffened in her chair. But she didn't scream. She didn't run. She held herself under icy control.

"I didn't . . . jeez, that came out wrong. We didn't . . . that is . . . we didn't intend to *actually* kill you. It's just that we were hired to. Or more accurately *I* was hired to kill you. It's just that James and I always travel together and, well, do stuff together."

"Even kill people," Mrs. Stout said calmly.

"Look, I didn't mean that the way it sounded. Honest. I, uh . . ."

"It was a case of mistaken identity," James said, finally speaking up, and in his normal tone and not that of the mushmouthed ignoramus that he sometimes put on as a disguise of sorts. "A man thought Dexter was some fellow named Chance Drewery, who we assume to be a hired killer. He paid Dex a lot of money, thinking Dex was this Drewery, and told him he'd get more once you were killed. But it was to look like an accident. He was very clear about that. Dex . . . or Drewery . . . was to kill you and make it look accidental. As it happens though, we aren't either one of us in the murdering business. So we came here today to find out more about what's going on. We wanted to warn you, and if the truth be told too we'd like to figure out some way to fleece the gentleman that wants you dead." James grinned. "We'd sort of like to keep his money and take some more of it if we can. But we'd as soon stop short of earning it honestly, if you know what I mean."

The girl surprised Dexter once again. Instead of falling into a trembling fit she began to laugh.

"Ma'am?"

"I like you. I like both of you. And I should thank you, of course, for turning down what I hope was a bountiful fee in exchange for my demise. Now, may I offer you some lunch . . . excuse me, I suppose it is getting on toward supper time, isn't it? but I'm a night person and don't usually have my breakfast until past noon . . . while you tell me the rest of this amazing story of yours."

"It isn't just a story, Mrs. Stout. It's the truth."

"Oh, I believe you. I suppose. But I would like to hear more of the details if you don't mind." She stood. "Come with me, please. I'm getting hungry. We can finish our talk in the dining room."

Dex and James followed in the young woman's wake, as obedient as a pair of schoolboys trudging along on their teacher's hem.

Pilar was waiting for them in a small but elegantly appointed dining room. Places were laid for four. Mrs. Stout sat at the head of the table with Dex and James on either side of her. Surprisingly—was there going to be *anything* about this woman that would prove normal? Dex wondered—Pilar sat down to the table service at the foot of the table.

• 21 •

"If you don't mind, gentlemen, we will postpone discussing your"—she smiled, —"business affairs. Until after dinner."

"Of course," Dex said. He wouldn't have expected anything else. One simply did not talk about matters of any weight or importance when one was at the table. "Would you please pass the butter, Pilar?"

Wilhelmina Stout began to giggle, the older woman to laugh.

"Did I say something wrong?"

"You said . . . oh, of course. The sound is so much like the Spanish name Pilar, isn't it?"

Dex blinked, not quite comprehending what she meant by that.

Wilhelmina reached forward and laid her fingertips gently on the back of Dex's wrist. He comprehended that well enough, thank you. Her touch was warm as a fresh foot brick. He began to get hard again.

"Forgive me. Both of you. Pilar is the word for 'mother' in our tongue. I haven't been calling her by name. That would be terribly rude. This is my mother, Edalyn. Pilar," she glanced at James and at Dex, "Mother, these gentlemen are the Yancey brothers, Dexter and James. I should have made all this clear before. I apologize."

"*Pilar* means mother," Dex said.

"That's right."

"And what language would that be?"

"Ki'iwa."

"Kiowa, did you say?"

"Oh, please. No! The Kiowa are a plains tribe. Very uncivilized, really. They live well west of here. We are the Ki'iwa. We're quite unrelated to them. Our people are a small tribe. We came from Asha'mingo, the coastal marshlands of what you call Mississippi—the state, that is, not the river."

"I see," Dex said, although in truth he was not entirely sure that he did understand.

"I'm told there once were many of us. More than a thousand. Now there would be . . ." She paused for a moment and asked something of her mother in a language that didn't even sound like words to Dex, never mind words that he could not understand but not really much like words at all. More a series of hisses and grunts.

Wilhelmina and her mother talked about it for several moments, then Wilhelmina said, "We think there are about two hundred forty or fifty Ki'iwa remaining. We adopted white ways when the French and the Spanish were still at Pensacola and Mobile. We welcomed the English and later you Americans. We became civilized and proud of it. It did no good, of course. We were Indians and we were in the way. We were removed from our beloved Asha'mingo in 1828 and given this land instead. Can you believe it? From swamp and marsh to this dry and barren country? But we are survivors, you see. And too few to think about warfare. We accepted our fate and rebuilt here.

"My late husband was a wonderful man, very strong and wise. He was already one of our principal leaders when the tribe was moved here. He set up our government, allocated our lands, established the laws and forestry methods that allow us to survive here."

Dex lifted an eyebrow. James said, "Forestry?"

Wilhelmina looked at him and nodded. "Our whole tribe depends on the production and sale of lumber. Oh, we have some grassland too, of course. In fact most of our reservation is grassland. We lease out grazing rights to a gentleman from Texas. That brings us a small amount of income. But most of our wealth . . . a poor choice of words, really, as we are anything but wealthy . . . most of our subsistence depends on forestry products. Lumber, turpentine, charcoal."

"I see," Dex said. He was perhaps beginning to.

"Our resources are limited, but then we have the advantage of being the only game in town, so to speak. We have the only timber available within many days' wagon travel. Anyone within several hundred miles who wants forestry products pretty much has to come to us."

"That sounds lucrative," Dex said.

Wilhelmina smiled again. "It does, doesn't it. But it really doesn't amount to all that much. For one thing, there just aren't all that many people who live in this rather empty country. For another, we very carefully limit our production.

"My husband established that practice deliberately and for more than one very good reason. One is that prices remain high when demand exceeds supply. That was one of his driving principles: Never allow the supply to quite meet the demand.

"And the other reason, even more compelling if harder for most people to see, is that our resources are very limited. Only a portion of the land here is capable of supporting timber. The water and soil conditions combine to take most of the land out of useful service for anything but a little grass. My husband was both wise and intelligent. He saw this and he put very stringent restrictions on the amount of timber the tribe can take from the mountains. And from the very first he insisted that two trees be planted for every one that is cut. We still do that, even since he passed away."

Dex frowned. There was a question he wanted to ask. But it would have to wait. It was related to Leroy Anderson and the fat man's desire to see Wilhelmina Stout dead, and it would have been impolite to bring that up until they were done dining.

Question? There would be quite a few questions to be asked from this point he thought.

He glanced across the table to James and saw that James too seemed preoccupied with serious thought while he toyed with the meal that had been placed before them.

Wilhelmina rattled and rambled informatively on, seemingly quite unaware of the sparks of interest she'd already created in her two guests.

·22·

They couldn't politely return to the subject of Wilhelmina's impending demise until after the meal, of course, but once they were back in the parlor with brandy and cigars for the gentlemen, sherry and minted confections for Wilhelmina and her mother, Dex lifted an eyebrow and glanced at James. He got a grin in return.

"Diamondbacks," James said softly, drawing the last sound out in a long, sibilant hiss.

"I agree," Dex said.

"Is there something I am missing?" Wilhelmina asked.

"Sort of," Dex admitted. "It's just, well, we sometimes like to sneak along unsuspected and strike fast."

"Snakes in the grass," James said.

"Sort of."

"Dexter and I were thinking, ma'am, that we would prefer to not kill you."

"If that is all right with you," Dex added with a perfectly solemn expression albeit with something of a twinkle to be found in his eye.

"I hope you won't mind telling me who it is who wants me dead," Wilhelmina said.

"Not at all. It's a neighbor of yours. A gent named Anderson."

The girl looked puzzled. "Mr. Leroy Anderson?"

"That's right." Dex noticed that the girl's mother seemed to be paying no particular attention to the conversation, despite the subject. He suspected that the older woman's command of English was not all that great, never mind how long the Ki'iwa tribe had been civilized.

"Mr. Anderson is the Texas gentleman I told you about earlier. He holds the grazing lease on the tribal lands. Why would he want me dead?"

"Why? That question pretty much always has a simple answer, miss, and usually it is the same one. Money. People who go to great and expensive lengths to get something done, especially something illegal like murder, always expect to gain from it. The possible reasons really aren't all that many though the details will vary," Dex told her, thinking it through pretty much as he spoke.

"Revenge is a good reason. Jealousy. A few more, perhaps. But mostly the answer to that question comes back to money."

"I still don't understand," the widow Stout said. "Mr. Anderson holds a five-year lease that was renewed by my husband not long before he died. The lease still has more than four years to run. And there weren't any negotiations to speak of when the new agreement was reached. We did not ask for more money and Mr. Anderson never said anything about wanting to pay less. He and George had worked out the terms of the original lease so that it would be fair to both parties. The renewal was mostly a matter of following the same form but with new dates. There was nothing complicated about it and nothing in dispute. It was all very straightforward."

"You're sure of that?" Dex asked. "There couldn't have been things said in the meetings that your husband didn't tell you about?"

"I am positive there weren't. For one thing, I was George's confidante. He told me everything. But apart from that, sir, I was also his amanuensis. And a member of the tribal council. I was personally present during all the meetings between my husband and Mr. Anderson. I heard every word that was spoken between them."

"So much for that theory," Dex said.

"You are a member of the council?" James asked, veering away from the subject at hand but seemingly amazed by the thought.

"Yes, of course."

"But . . ."

Wilhelmina smiled. "But I am a woman. Is that it?"

James nodded. "Meaning no offense, but . . . yes, ma'am."

"The Ki'iwa do not discriminate. Not about gender and not about race. I'd hoped you would have discovered that for yourself by now."

"Oh, I have. Everyone has treated me fine here. I just didn't know . . . you know . . . that it would apply to women too."

"Very much so. After George died, I was elected to replace him as President of the council. Mostly as a matter of respect for George, of course. But it is also true that I have more experience in council meetings than anyone else now in office. I began attending them as George's secretary even before he became a widower and asked me to become his wife."

"You must have been very young."

"But capable," Wilhelmina said in a voice that was soft enough but which had steel barely hidden beneath that velvet surface.

"I wouldn't doubt that for a moment," Dex assured her.

"This is all very interesting," James said, "but it sure doesn't give us any idea why Anderson would want the lady killed. Especially why he'd want it to look like an accident."

"So you were hired to kill me?" the girl said. "And it is to seem an accident?"

"Apparently that's all-important," Dex affirmed. "It's why he wanted to pay for a specialist like this Chance Drewery . . . whom he thinks I am . . . instead of having one of his own people sneak around and do the job."

"Am I at least worth a great deal of money?" Wilhelmina asked.

"Three thousand," Dex told her.

"Plus expenses," James said.

"And a bonus if no one questions that it was really an accidental death."

"How odd."

"Exactly," Dex said.

"And if you don't mind me asking, sir, how is it that you expect to earn your fee?"

"To tell you the truth, miss, we aren't entirely sure about that."

"But I think it's safe to say that we aren't honest," James said with a chuckle. "We don't intend to earn our pay by performing the job to our, um, employer's specification."

"Thank goodness for that." The girl said something to her mother in the Ki'iwa tongue and the older woman laughed.

"Diamondbacks," Dex said.

"We'll think of something," James said. "Fortunately we have a little time to work with. Anderson said the job should be done by the end of next month. By the thirtieth day of June actually. Or any time before that."

"The tribal council will meet again the first week of July," Wilhelmina said.

"Then that's sure to have something to do with it," Dex said.

"But I can't imagine what. The grazing lease won't be discussed again for years. And there is nothing else on the table that would involve Mr. Anderson in any way."

"Damned odd," Dex said. "I guess that's just another thing we'll want to learn more about while we're trying to figure a way around this."

Dex paused, and then had a burst of true inspiration.

"In the meantime," he said, "I'll want to make sure Anderson knows that I'm on the job and hard at work looking for a way to, um, earn my pay."

"Yes?"

"I think what we'd best do, miss, is for me to make a show of sparking you."

"I beg your pardon?"

"Anyone with eyes can see that you are an exceptionally pretty woman. Surely no one would think it strange if a gentleman newly acquainted with you should fall in love and want to pay court. You know. Take drives along the creek. Go on picnics and long rides in the hills. Like that."

Dex didn't have to look at James to see the sour reaction his plan would be receiving from that direction. Dex paying public court to Wilhelmina Stout would pretty much cut James's opportunities right out of the picture.

"Yes, I see," the widow Stout said pensively. "Yes, I suppose that does make sense. And Mr. Anderson would view your attentions as a matter of his hired assassin seeking a chance to murder me under the guise of accident." She seemed to think about the plan for a moment. Then she smiled. "Yes, I agree that is what we should do, Mr. Yancey."

"Dex. You should call me Dex, I think, if we're to become an item of local gossip."

"You will, I hope, keep me updated on your plans for murderous methods," she said.

"Be glad to," he said with a laugh.

♦ 23 ♦

"There has to be a way for Anderson to profit from your death," James said abruptly. Dex suspected James was eager to get off the subject of Dexter wooing the lovely Wilhelmina Stout and back onto something more agreeable. Like mayhem.

"I truly cannot imagine what that would be," the lady responded.

Dex looked around. The house was not large but it was elegant. "You obviously have money," he said.

The comment drew a most unladylike snort from Wilhelmina.

"Was that a laugh or did some sherry just go up your nose?" Dex asked.

"God, I can hardly wait to be alone with you, Mr. Yancey. You're *such* a charmer."

He grinned.

"What you said was more than enough to make me laugh though."

"And how is that?" he asked.

"That we are wealthy." She shook her head and smiled. "We are hardly that. No more so than anyone else in the tribe."

Dex made a show of once again peering about him. The house itself was lovely and the appointments done with exquisite taste.

"This is not my house," Wilhelmina said.

"But I thought . . ."

"The house, the sawmill, the land . . . all of it belongs to the Ki'iwa people. We do not hold property as individuals. We never have. My mother and I moved in here when I married George. We remain here thanks to my election as President of the tribal council. When I relinquish that title, the new president will take possession of this house. It is a . . . I suppose you could say it is a tangible symbol of the office. Or a perquisite if you would prefer.

"As for money, mother and I each receive an equal share of the tribal income. Just like every other Ki'iwa. We get no more and no less."

"What about profits?" James asked. "You said money from the grazing lease all goes into one pot. But what about the profit from individual business? Like, I don't know, like the hotel, for instance?"

"That income, the income from each of us, belongs to the tribe as a whole. Have you noticed there is no bank in our town?"

Dex hadn't. But he did not want to say so. He remained mute.

"We have no need for a bank since we have no need for loans or savings or any of that."

"And foodstuffs? Clothing or thread and needles, things like that?" James persisted.

"We use cash for our purchases, of course. We all receive the same amounts but we may choose to spend differently. We can buy whatever we want or need just like anyone else. But actual property, houses and stores and the like, those all belong to the tribe. There is virtually no individual ownership of real property."

"It's . . . a strange system," Dex said.

The girl smiled again and said something to her mother before she responded to him. "It works," she said at length. "To tell you the truth, I doubt that our system would do for a larger group. Certainly it wouldn't do at all for an entire nation like the United States. Greed and human nature would intrude. But here . . ." She spread her palms and smiled. "We know each other intimately. We trust each other. All of our needs are met."

The mother interrupted briefly. Wilhelmina nodded and added, "Pilar . . . Mother, that is . . . reminds me to explain to you that we Ki'iwa are taught literally from birth to act cooperatively. It would be shameful for any of us to do anything that would be harmful to the tribe."

"Idyllic," Dex said.

"Yes, it is."

"But it sure makes it more difficult for me to understand why Anderson would want you dead. You've never offended him or . . . anything like that that you can think of?"

The girl shook her head. "Never. I've spoken to him, of course. But only in casual pleasantries. I've never had a serious discussion with him."

Dex grunted. He could see that James was just as puzzled as he. After a moment Dex rose. James did likewise.

"Thank you for the meal, Miz Stout. And for the information."

"If we are to be sweethearts, Dex . . . you did say I should call you that, I believe . . . if we are to be sweethearts I think it best that you call me by name, don't you?"

"Right, Wilhelmina."

She chuckled. "Willie. All my friends call me Willie."

"And your sweethearts?"

The amusement died and for a moment Dex thought he'd inadvertently said something insulting. Then she spoke again and he realized that what he saw in her pretty face was instead a deep and unspoken sorrow. "I would rather you not use the pet names George and I shared, please."

"Of course. I'm . . . sorry."

Apparently her marriage to a much, much older man had been a match with genuine affection in it.

"Thank you for coming, gentlemen." Her moment of sorrow was put behind her and she smiled again. She stepped forward to grasp James's hand and squeeze it, then Dexter's. "I know I can count on you both," she said.

"Damned trusting filly, isn't she?" James observed when they were well away from the house and on their way back to the Ki'iwa—and who the hell would have thought the sign was spelled correctly about that—hotel.

"How's that?" Dex asked.

"Three thousand is an awful lot of money to walk away from."

"There's nobody I know that's thinking about walking away from it," Dex protested. "Me, I'm thinking in terms of collecting that second half and the bonus payment besides."

James gave him an odd look but didn't say anything. In fact James didn't speak again the whole way back to the hotel.

• 24 •

Dex and James wandered off to the saloon later that evening. Neither was particularly hungry after the meal they'd had with Willie Stout and her mother, but a night spent in a lonely hotel room was not particularly appealing. Dex figured a drink and a nibble at the free lunch spread would not be amiss.

The barroom was not empty, but it was far from being crowded. There were only a handful of customers present when they arrived. Seven, actually. Dex counted. Four men were grouped around a card table toward the rear of the place. Three men were leaning on the bar. Most of the men, three of those who were playing cards and one standing at the bar, had the dark, broad features that indicated they were Indians of some sort, presumably Ki'iwa.

Dex idly wondered if the saloon too was owned by the tribe. If indeed it would be legal for an Indian tribe to own and operate a bar since by law they were not allowed to drink alcohol. Would it necessarily follow that they could not profit from it as well?

"What will it be, gents?" the bartender asked. Dex was not sure if he were Indian or not. He could as easily have been Italian, Greek or any number of other possibilities.

"Brandy for me," Dex said.

"Beer," James told him.

The olive-skinned barman nodded and went to fill their orders.

A door at the back of the room opened, and a small woman entered. She had a very dark complexion and a flat nose. Her figure was squat and dumpy. She would not have been outstanding in any way. Except one.

The woman had a set of tits on her that would have done justice to a Brown Swiss. The cow, that is. Hell, she could have competed neck and neck with a *pair* of Brown Swiss udders.

Dex considered it a remarkable achievement for her to walk upright without assistance. At the very least she should've been pushing a handcart before her to take the weight of those monstrous knockers.

James goggled at the sight. "I think," he said, "I'm in love."

"Unrequited love is a dangerous thing," Dex told him.

"Yeah. If nothing else, my man, it makes a fellow's balls hurt."

"That could be distracting."

"Dangerous, I believe you said."

"It would be best for both of us if you were to at least inquire as to the, um, lady's plans for the remainder of the evening."

There was not much question as to the big/little woman's purpose in being there. Her overly rouged cheeks, skirt short enough to put her ankles on public display and predatory manner when looking over the customers made that quite clear.

"When the man brings that beer," James said, "tell him not to save it for me. I don't expect to be back."

Dex grinned and gave his friend a wink, and James hurried toward the back of the saloon before someone else could get to the busty little broad before him.

The bartender brought their drinks moments later. Shrugging, Dex dumped his brandy into what would have been James's beer, then paid for both of them.

The bartender offered no comment.

For a moment Dex was tempted to ask if the trollop's profits would also be passed along into the tribal treasury. Fortunately that moment passed, and he contented himself with a swallow of the wicked but indeed quite tasty beer.

· 25 ·

"You would be Mr. Milton, I presume?"

Dex looked at the man who'd spoken to him. He was fairly sure he had never seen this fellow before. The man was dark of hair, complexion and eye coloring and probably was a Ki'iwa although he held a mug of some foamy beverage in his hand. "Yes, and you would be . . . ?"

The Indian smiled and extended his hand to Dex. "Bob Hatchet," he said.

"Hatchet," Dex repeated. "Like the, um . . ."

The smile got even bigger as merriment sparked in Bob Hatchet's eyes. "Yes. Just like that kind of hatchet. But please don't worry. I haven't whacked anyone with one of my grandfather's namesakes in ever so long."

Dex laughed. "Sorry. I didn't mean to be rude."

"You weren't. Just a little confused, that's all."

"There aren't so many Indians where I'm from," Dex explained. Although that probably was quite unnecessary.

"And that would be?"

"Louisiana," Dex told him.

Hatchet nodded. "That makes us practically neighbors."

"So I understand. I believe the tribe is from Mississippi?"

"Asha'mingo," Hatchet corrected.

"Thanks. I'd heard the name but couldn't recall it."

"You know the name?" Hatchet seemed surprised.

Dex shook his head quickly. "Not from before. Mrs. Stout mentioned it to me this afternoon."

"Oh, you know our Willie, do you?"

"We've only met. A mutual acquaintance asked me to pay his respects."

"I see. Did the lady mention that she is President of our tribal council?"

"She did but more or less in passing."

Bob Hatchet turned to the bartender and made a circular motion to call for another round. "You'll permit me to buy you another, I hope," the Indian said to Dexter.

"You're very kind."

The bartender came over and asked, "Do you want both again?" He motioned to the beer mug and empty glass the brandy had been in. Dex shook his head. "Just a brandy, please."

"And another sarsaparilla for you, Bob?"

"Please."

Which explained the foamy beverage. No alcohol. Dex gathered that the liquor laws here allowed Indians to frequent saloons. They just couldn't drink in them.

"How did you know my name?" Dex asked while they waited for the drinks.

"Oh, we have few secrets in a community this small, Mr. Milton. But if you really want to know, Eugene told me."

"Eugene?"

"Eugene Duckwing." When that drew no comprehension, Hatchet added, "Eugene runs the hotel where you and Mr. Emory are staying."

"I see. Thank you. And what is it that you do, Mr. Hatchet?"

"Bob. Please call me Bob. Everyone does. As for your question, I am supervisor at the sawmill. I'm sure you noticed it when you called on Willie today."

"I did indeed. I didn't walk through it but from the distance it certainly looked well operated."

"You flatter me, sir."

"Nothing that I didn't think earned," Dex lied. Well, fibbed really. He was only being polite.

"And your business, Mr. Milton?"

"At the moment, I am but a wanderer. Some second sons," Dex was in fact the older of a pair of twins, but he certainly didn't intend to get into all that with a stranger, "take a tour of the continent when their time comes to explore the world. I thought it would be more interesting to see our own country first. Someday I still may want to see Europe and the ancient world. First I intend to see all the wonders this country has to offer."

"I envy you the opportunity," Hatchet said. "I've always wanted to travel." The smile returned. "So far the closest I've come is my collection of stereopticon views. Perhaps you'd like to see them sometime."

"Perhaps I would," Dex said. Now that one was a definite lie. It left fibbing in the dust. If there was any prospect guaranteed to bore him it would be to sit around in some stranger's parlor staring at a bunch of dusty photographs. Even stereoptical ones that feigned three dimensional depth.

"I have views from London. Paris. Egypt and the pyramid tombs of the great pharaohs."

"Really," Dex said, trying his best to put a note of interest into his tone of voice.

"Oh, they are really quite grand, I assure you. You would be welcome to view them any time, Mr. Milton. Any time at all."

"You're very kind, Mr. Hatchet."

"Bob. Please call me Bob."

Bob seemed to be quite thoroughly amused by something; Dex wasn't sure by what but he had the nagging suspicion that Hatchet's pleasure derived from the prospect of a new victim for the tortures of his stereopticon. Dex suppressed a shudder and drank back his brandy rather more quickly than he otherwise might have.

"Would you care for another?" Bob offered. "It would be my pleasure, believe me."

"Thank you, Mi . . . Bob, I mean. Thank you, Bob. You are most generous. But I'm getting tired. I do hope I'll see you again though." Dex took half a step back away from the bar.

"Please do. And if you want to see my views, just drop by. No special invitation is needed. Just come by and rap on the door. You can ask anyone where I live. They'll tell you."

"Thanks, Bob. Really." Dex smiled. And beat a hasty retreat back to the hotel where he might find a bit of solitude . . . and not one single stereopticon card.

· 26 ·

There was no sign of the desk clerk Eugene Duckwing when Dex arrived at the hotel. He let himself in at the unlocked front door and was started up the stairs. He was halfway up when he heard Duckwing come out of the little office that lay behind the counter area.

"Mr. Milton?"

Dex stopped. "Yes?"

"I have a note here for you, sir."

"All right, thanks." Dex went back down and retrieved a small envelope from Duckwing. He was careful not to open it there in the lobby, however. It might well have been—in fact probably was—a message from Leroy Anderson. After all, how many people did he know in Ki'iwa anyway?

Once safely inside his room, though, and with the lamp turned high he broke open the waxed seal—the design impressed into the sealing wax was unfamiliar to him—and found, "In view of our sudden attraction to each other, Mr. Milton, kindly do me the honor of joining me for a picnic on the morrow. Come at noon, if you please. I shall have a breakfast prepared."

No, the note was not in fact from Anderson. Dex thought

the prospect of a picnic with Wilhelmina Stout much more attractive than one with the fat man would have been.

Dex woke fairly late in the morning and found James still so soundly asleep he looked like he was in a coma. Dex had rather dimly heard James come creeping in sometime around dawn-thirty. It had been a long night and presumably a good one.

Dex dressed quietly so as not to disturb poor, worn-out James and went downstairs. Eugene Duckwing was behind the counter.

"Good morning, Mr. Milton."

"Good morning, Eugene." Duckwing seemed not to find it at all remarkable that Dex would know his name.

"Your carriage will be ready about a quarter till twelve if that's all right," Duckwing offered.

"Pardon me? Carriage?"

"Yes, sir. For the picnic."

"But how . . ."

Duckwing grinned. "She sent me a note too, sir. Asking for the use of the carriage, you see. We all share in the use of it."

"I see," Dex said, beginning to. Small town? This one pretty much took the cake when it came to everyone knowing everyone else's business.

He thanked Eugene Duckwing and wandered off in search of something to hold body and soul together until time for the widow Stout's post-noon breakfast, then piddled the remainder of the morning away by walking down along the creek—never mind that the Ki'iwa insisted it was a river, the damn thing couldn't possibly be considered that by anyone who'd grown up on the banks of the Mississippi—and at the appointed time returned to the hotel.

There was, as promised, an old but still fairly nice open landau parked in the street at the front of the hotel. It was pulled by a single gray with a maroon plume bobbing grandly above its headstall. The color of the plume was the exact same shade as the bodywork of the landau. It was a

nice touch, Dex conceded as he went inside to confirm—
he would hate like hell to be arrested for horse theft—that
this was indeed the rig the Ki'iwa tribe shared among themselves and that he should hop in and drive it away.

• 27 •

"This is lovely," Dex said. He meant it. There was a line of greenery along the creek that appeared unbroken, the foliage thick and lush even though the land around it was brown and sere. "I'm surprised to see so many trees. Up there too." He pointed toward the hillsides where the forest seemed also thick. "You've been cutting timber around here for years now. I would've thought it would all be cut away for an awful distance by now."

"I told you. George was a very careful husbandman. We cut very selectively, and we always replant more than we take out. That way we will always have our livelihood intact. Turn here, please."

Dex did, guiding the landau in the direction Wilhelmina pointed. Once they were off the road the ironclad wheels rumbled and grumbled over sun-baked earth and a scattering of stones.

"In there. Just to the left of that big tree."

"All right." He sneaked a quick look at the widow Stout. She was even lovelier today than the day before. She had her hair pinned into a bun and covered by a cream-colored bonnet. The effect was to draw attention to the planes of her cheeks, the depth of her eyes and the slenderness of her neck. Dex was not sure but he thought she had applied a hint of makeup as well. Damn but she was one fine-looking woman.

Her figure, however, was completely hidden. Presumably because of the dust of travel she had dressed for the picnic in a voluminous duster that covered her from throat to ankle. The sleeves were tucked into the wide, gauntletlike cuffs of her gloves. Duster and gloves alike were a slightly darker shade of cream than the bonnet. A puff of scarf—silk, he thought—acted on behalf of modesty at the vee above the top button of her duster. Dex was not a great admirer of modesty as a trait desirable in women. He found it to be especially distressing today. A form-fitting dress would have been much more to his liking than an all-covering duster.

Still, she would surely remove the duster when they got wherever they were going.

"Now between those trees, if you please, and on down to the riverbank," she directed.

As they left the open grassland and entered the leafy shelter of the woods along the creek he could feel the temperature drop. Somehow it seemed quieter inside the thicket also. Quieter and more . . . peaceful.

Dex grunted softly and reasoned that of course it seemed quieter in the wood. Because in fact it was quieter. The wheels crunched loudly over hardpack earth out in the open. Here inside the cool shade of the riverbank the tires rolled over decaying leaves and soft loam. Naturally it was quieter. There wasn't anything at all special about it.

"Yes?" Wilhelmina asked in response to the sound he made.

Dex shook his head. "Nothing. Sorry."

She didn't pursue the question, merely directed him further, finally instructing him to park beneath a particular tree and to back the rig in so they were facing southwest.

"I hope you are hungry," she said when the carriage was positioned to her satisfaction and a drop weight had been clipped to the gray's bit.

"I am," he said as he handed her down to the ground

and reached into the pack for the wicker hamper she'd brought along.

The statement was true enough. But incomplete. Dex's hunger had nothing to do with food and quite a lot to do with the widow Wilhelmina Stout. She would, he thought, make a most delectable mouthful.

"Over here, please." She already had her lap robe in hand and was busy spreading and tidying it on a flat, bare bit of ground from which one could see the creek.

Sunlight filtering through the branches overhead dappled the moving water, sparkling and dancing gaily.

A rod or two downstream there must have been a riffle or small rapid because Dex could hear the water chuckle. He could not see whatever the obstruction was, but the sound was delightful, merry and soothing at the same time. He liked it.

Come to think of it, he noticed while Wilhelmina opened the hamper and began unpacking an array of finger foods, from this lovely spot it was impossible to see anything outside the woods—out onto the road, for instance—or anything much at all except the creek, the trees and a screen of rather dense underbrush. If the girl hadn't told him how to get here he never would have thought to find such isolation. And within two miles of the town too. He stood, his feet planted in soft, lush, sweet smelling grass, and looked about with satisfaction. He liked it here.

"Breakfast is ready," Wilhelmina said.

Dex turned back to face her. And was immediately disappointed. She hadn't chosen to remove the damned duster after all. Oh well. Likely she was still feeling too cool after the heat out in the open. For now there was the prospect of food. That would do. It would have to.

He sat across the robe from Wilhelmina and reached for a pecan roll that was crusty-gooey with baked-on butter and brown sugar and cinnamon.

· 28 ·

"Satisfied?" Wilhelmina asked.

"Yes, thank you." And so he was. More or less. Certainly the food had been satisfactory, consisting mostly of sweet-breads, hard boiled eggs and thin, crispy slivers of cold bacon. His disappointment came from the fact that Wilhel-mina continued to wear the damned all-covering duster.

The widow carefully retrieved all the leftover goodies from the blanket where they sat, packed everything back into the hamper and latched the wicker lid closed. She set the hamper aside with a sigh. "Personally, Dexter, I am not at all satisfied."

He frowned. "Is there something I can get you?"

"Of course there is." She stood.

Dex jumped to his feet also. "I'm sorry, I . . ."

"Shhh." She placed a finger to her lips—very soft and full lips they were, he noted—to shush him. He shushed.

Wilhelmina Stout, President of the Ki'iwa tribal council, kicked off her shoes—soft, loose-fitting half-boots actu-ally—and pulled the scarf from around her neck, allowing it to drop from her fingers and float gently to earth. She pulled her bonnet off, and her hair spilled sleek and gleam-ing to her waist. She unbuttoned the duster and with a shrug of her shoulders let it slither from her to fall in a puddle of cream-colored cloth around her feet.

With those few articles missing, the only thing Wilhelmina wore was a smile.

A rather smug smile at that, Dex thought.

And once again his pecker began doing battle with the buttons of his fly.

He thought the girl was pretty when she was dressed? That had been only a hint of the beauty that was concealed beneath the wrappings.

"That tickles," Willie said, her voice a hoarse and husky whisper.

"D'you want me to stop?"

"God, no." She shuddered as his lips traced lightly up and down the soft surfaces of her throat while his fingers stroked and teased somewhat to the south of there.

Dex lifted his head. Smiled and gave her a gentle kiss on the lips, then moved down to nuzzle and suckle at her nipples, which were small and dark and sharp-pointed. Willie moaned and began to wriggle her hips in small, involuntary movements.

"Dexter, dear."

"Mmm?"

"There is something . . . something my husband taught me. Something very special."

"Yes?"

He stopped what he was doing and looked at her. He wasn't entirely sure but he thought the girl was blushing just a little.

"My husband. He was an older man, you know."

"Yes, I know that."

"He was wonderful and I loved him dearly, and he pleased me greatly. But George couldn't get . . . you know . . . a very good hard-on. He loved sex and taught me to love it too. But his erections weren't very hard and didn't last all that long. But there was never a night . . . or a day . . . that he couldn't satisfy me. If you know what I mean."

"I'm not sure that I do." Having a limp dick was not a

problem Dex himself had ever had to overcome.

"He . . . well . . . he used . . . this is embarrassing."

"It's all right. Tell me."

"If you think it is disgusting I won't hold it against you."

"Dear girl, I count on the hope that you will indeed hold it against me." He smiled and kissed her again. "Your body, that is."

Willie was most definitely blushing now. "I found that I really like . . . that is to say I climax if . . . damn it, Dexter, have you ever used your . . . um . . . your tongue? On a woman's body, that is?"

Dex grinned. "Is that all? Hell, why didn't you say so."

He shifted position appropriately, and Willie eagerly opened herself to him.

Her pubic hair was jet black and very dense. The individual hairs were fairly short and straight, without a hint of curl or curve. They were, he discovered, already softened by a flow of clear moisture that glistened in the sunlight.

He dipped his head. Stopped. Allowed the warmth of his breath to touch her first. She smelled clean and fresh.

Tasted just as fresh and clean. When he kissed her there a soft, barely audible groan escaped from her lips and she reached down to touch the back of his head, urging him on.

Dex obliged, paying court to her with lip and tongue. Playing, teasing, roving across wet, pink, quivering woman-flesh.

Willie began to grunt and her hips to gyrate. Her breath quickened and her fingers clenched tight on his hair as her excitement grew and grew and soon exploded in a convulsive spasm of sheer pleasure.

She screamed, the sound of her cry sharp and small in the stillness of the outdoors.

A moment later she collapsed, utterly spent.

Dex planted one final kiss onto the plump, thoroughly drenched lips of her pussy and withdrew, running a line of kisses across her belly, briefly onto each firm, small breast and over her throat until finally he reached her mouth. Willie smiled.

"Is that what you had in mind?" he teased.

She sighed. "Approximately from the moment I opened that door and saw you standing there," she whispered with a smile.

"Lucky me," he said.

"Lucky me," she echoed.

She reached for his pecker—the poor damned thing was so ready it was bouncing and bumping with every beat of his heart; so over-ready it was beginning to ache from the continued excitement without release—and with a gentle tug encouraged him toward her wet and waiting sex.

⋄ 29 ⋄

"Thank you."

Dex was quite frankly startled. He turned his head and gave the girl a sharp look, but he would have sworn there was no sarcasm in either her voice or her expression. She'd said it and apparently she'd meant it. But it did not seem entirely normal that the woman should thank the man for a bout of—admittedly exceptional—lovemaking.

Willie smiled at him. She looked relaxed now. Happy. Satisfied.

Well, so was he. The girl was a dynamo of vitality when in action. Thrusting, demanding, clutching, in her passion even biting at times. Dex was fairly sure she'd left marks on his shoulders and probably scratches on his back as well.

He'd enjoyed receiving every one of them.

Thank you, indeed.

He smiled back at her and dipped his chin a fraction of an inch so he could kiss her.

"Are you in a hurry to get back?" he asked, hoping she was not.

"No. Are you?"

He shook his head.

Willie rolled her pretty head to the side and ran the tip

of her tongue across Dex's throat. He shivered with pleasure.

"I like the feel of the air on my skin," the president of the Ki'iwa council said. "I love being naked outdoors." She laughed. "It must be the Indian in me."

"It's me in the Indian that I like best," Dex countered. Willie laughed again and shifted onto her side, throwing one arm across his chest and burrowing her face into his armpit.

"Are you sure you can breathe in there?"

"Of course."

"If I'd known about this I would have taken another bath this morning."

"Don't be silly. I like the smell of a man. Like the taste of one too. I'm only sorry I wasn't able to take you in my mouth. Tomorrow maybe?" She sounded hopeful.

But then so was he. The idea that she would welcome a repeat engagement was encouraging indeed. "Is there some reason why we can't give you a sample this afternoon still? You said you don't need to hurry back to town."

Willie blinked. Then appeared to comprehend. "With my husband, once a day was all he could manage. He loved it. So did I to tell you the truth. But there were only a few times when George could manage more than once. Is it so very different with a young man then?"

"I expect so."

"Good." She sounded pleased.

"I don't mean to offend, but . . . could I ask you a rather personal question?"

"Of course."

"I sort of thought . . . that is, I assumed . . . I mean, coming straight to this isolated spot and everything . . ."

Willie laughed. "You mean you assumed that I was . . . am . . . promiscuous."

"That isn't the way I would have put it."

"But it is what you meant, yes?"

He nodded. Reluctantly.

Willie spotted a trickle of sweat on his chest and paused to lick it away, then spoke. "I was completely faithful to my husband, Dexter. I loved him. I was a virgin when I came to his bed, and I knew no other man for as long as George lived. After he died, I was lonely. But it wouldn't do for me to start allowing other members of the tribe into my bed. Not that some of them haven't tried. I take that as a compliment. But not much of one. It could be that they really just want a favor from me because of my position. At any rate it would only create potential difficulties. I try to be impartial. I have to be.

"And as for others," she shrugged. "There was one man. A white man from St. Louis. He is a salesman dealing in hardware. We buy materials for the sawmill and other equipment from him sometimes. He is a nice looking man. Clean. He is also married. I let him lure me into bed. He was . . . not nearly so much fun to be with as you are. Not nearly as good, you see. And with him there was no love. My love for George made me happy to please him. With the salesman," she shook her head, "I felt shamed afterward. It was awkward trying to do business with him. He expected me to be grateful, I think; he wanted me to place big orders and not question his prices. When I refused, he claimed I only fucked him with my body so I could fuck him in business. That experience was not . . . nice. If you see what I mean."

"No, that wouldn't be. Not at all."

"He and George and now you. That is the sum and total of my experience, sir."

"For a lass with so little experience, ma'am, you display amazing aptitude and natural abilities." Dex laughed and kissed her again.

"La, sir, I thank you for the lovely compliment. You are too kind."

"And you, m'lady, are too lovely." Dex could feel an arousal of fresh interest after the brief rest. He cupped her breast, small and taut and slightly rubbery in his hand, and gently massaged it, rolling her nipple between his thumb and forefinger while his tongue explored within her mouth.

Willie's hand found his cock and she began to manipulate him. For a girl who claimed to be unskilled she was damn-all able.

As Dex became hard again, the Indian girl disengaged from his embrace and began slowly, thoroughly licking him, her tongue roving from one of Dexter's nipples to the other and back again, then lower and lower still.

She ran her tongue up one side of his shaft, swirled the engorged head of his cock inside her mouth and then licked her way down again to his balls.

She'd said she wanted the taste of him. Dex was more than willing to give it to her.

Willie was not without desires of her own, however. While she noisily and quite happily sucked and slurped, she raised herself over him, placing one slim thigh tight against each of Dex's ears and positioning her pink, dripping wet labia close to his chin.

Subtle, Dex thought. The damned girl was really subtle, all right.

Not that he held the unspoken request against her. A girl who was this talented surely had the right to expect a little pleasure in return.

Besides, sixty-nine is a perfectly lovely number. The most enjoyable number of all, Dex thought.

He gave himself over to the sensations he was giving. And even more so to the ones he was getting.

◆ 30 ◆

"**O**uch!" Dex snapped upright at the sudden sharp sting. His forehead collided with the shelf of Willie's jaw, sending the girl tumbling onto her pretty butt with a yelp of her own. "What'd you do that for?" he complained, rubbing his chest.

Willie laughed and, still naked, scrambled on hands and knees to regain the blanket where they'd had their picnic and other pleasures. Damn girl had yanked one of his chest hairs out. It hurt. A little. Mostly it had startled the hell out of him.

"You fell asleep," she accused.

"So?"

"It is rude for a gentleman to sleep in the presence of a lady."

"I had a good excuse."

"Yes?"

"You wore me out," he said with a grin.

Willie seemed unimpressed with that argument. "It was rude of you," she insisted. "Besides, I want to talk."

"There are better ways to wake a man," he told her.

"Umm, I can think of a few at that," she said with an impish smile.

"Next time try one of those, will you please?"

"Maybe."

"And if it wouldn't be too personal and offend you, may I tell you something?"

"You have leave to do so," she said in a mock-formal voice.

"You have some twigs and stuff on your ass now."

"Ooo!" She jumped up, stepped off the blanket and vigorously brushed herself off—she indeed had had bits and pieces of forest litter clinging to her butt—then rejoined him on the blanket. Dex rewarded her with a long, lingering kiss. He liked this girl. Quite a lot.

"So what d'you want to talk about that's so important you have to rip half my chest off to get my attention?"

"It was one hair. One tiny hair."

"Look. I'm bleeding."

"There isn't even a red mark there."

"No, I'm bleeding. I'm sure of it."

She kissed his chest, missing the place where she'd snatched the hair but finding a nipple instead.

"That's much better," he agreed. "Thank you."

"Good. Now are you finally ready to be serious?" she asked.

"If I have to. Now that I'm awake."

"I've been thinking," she said.

"So have I." He reached out and gave her left tit a playful tweak.

"Later. Be serious now. Please."

Dex sobered. "All right."

"I've been thinking about this job of yours. Have you come up with any solutions yet?"

Dex shook his head. "No, not one. James and I talked about it last night some, but we don't have any firm ideas yet."

"I think I do," Willie said. "Mama and I have talked about it too, of course. And we have something of an advantage. We know the country around here and the people so we have a better idea of what we have available to work with."

"You don't have to offer any explanations or apologies if that's what you are up to. I don't mind hearing a good idea even if it does come from a woman."

She kissed him and laid her head against his chest. "Good. Most of the white men I've known don't think a woman has a brain."

Dex grinned. "I think you'll find that most of us concede, though, that you women have pussies. Much more useful than a brain any old time."

"Hush. I'm trying to be serious here."

"Yes, ma'am."

"Mr. Anderson hired you to kill me. And to make it look like an accident. Isn't that right?"

"Yes, it is."

"So the answer Mama and I came up with is perfectly obvious, Dexter."

"Yes?"

"You will just have to kill me, that's all."

She gave him a bright and cheerful smile and sat back onto her heels, beaming with the obviousness and simplicity of her solution.

· 31 ·

"By God," Dex said, "I don't believe I've ever met a woman more accommodating and agreeable than that. And I can understand it. You are so pleased with the way I make love that you would do anything for me. Of course. There's one part that puzzles me though and that's why your mother would agree to it too. Or does she want to be next in line for my body when you are, as they say, beyond the Great Divide?"

"I don't mean *kill me* kill me. I just mean you should . . . kill me."

"I hope to hell you don't expect me to understand that," Dex said.

Willie laughed. "None of us knows what possible reason Mr. Anderson could have for wanting me dead. After all, we're almost strangers. And he has never approached the council with any sort of request that George would not have approved of. Or that I wouldn't now that I'm council President. Mama and I talked about this a lot last night, and we can't think of anything . . . not one single thing . . . that would explain the idea of Mr. Anderson hiring someone to kill me." She smiled quite prettily.

"What we came up with," she said, "is the idea that if

Mr. Anderson believes you have completed your job, he will then do whatever it is he has in mind, whatever it is that requires me to be out of the way. Do you see?"

"Indeed I do," Dex agreed. "But how am I supposed to kill you, and make it seem an accident, and not have anyone question—how am I supposed to do all this without having to produce a body?"

Willie gave him a smug look. "That is where our particular knowledge comes in, you see. I will have my little accident while we are on one of our outings. By now the whole tribe knows about this picnic, of course. There will have to be more of them. If you don't mind, that is." She giggled just a little.

"I think I can bear up under the strain," he said with a straight face. While staring at the glossy black bush at her crotch.

"Yes, I'm sure we can find ways to pass the time," Willie agreed. "But back to our plan. We will go on several of our picnics, you see. The tribe will simply think you are courting me. And Mr. Anderson, if he hears about it, will almost certainly assume that you are devising a way to murder me."

"Of course," Dex agreed.

"Then one fine afternoon there will be a tragedy. A fall. I might be wading in the river, perhaps. Standing on a rock. I could slip and fall and hit my head on the rock, you see."

"That much is easy. But what about the body?"

Willie's smile did not lessen. "You will rush back to town, of course. And naturally you will stop at the first place you come to. Which will be my house. You will oh so frantically tell my mother. And Pilar, Mother that is, will just as naturally want to take charge of my body in the proper Ki'iwa manner. She will wrap the body and take it onto the mountain. She will put it on a scaffold and offer up sacrifices and chants. Then she will come back and tell everyone what happened. And everyone will hear from my mother's own lips the sad tale of the accident and the burial.

"The council members will go back to the mountain with my mother. They will bring symbolic gifts for me to take with me into the next world, and they will offer chants and ritual prayers. Oh, it will be very sad. Very solemn. As a white man you won't be able to be there for that. But I know you will be very sad too. You will miss me."

"Indeed I shall," Dex agreed. "But . . . you say these council members will have to go up and see the body too?"

"Don't forget, Dexter, I also said that Mama will have to wrap her darling daughter's body ready for burial. We will build the scaffold and we will prepare the burial in all the proper ways except one. Inside the wrappings we will put some sticks and rocks and things. Something to give the shape of the body, that's all."

"And you will be . . . ?"

"At the wood-cutting camp," Willie said, as if that explained everything. To Dex it didn't explain anything. He raised an eyebrow and waited for her to go on.

"I told you, we are very careful to limit what we take from our available resources. Each fall we mark the trees we intend to cut. We do the actual cutting during the fall and early winter, when there will be snow on the ground to help slide the logs downhill. In spring we plant seedlings for our future use. And in the springtime too when the river is at its highest we float the logs we've been drying through the deepest winter. There is a period of only a week or so when the river carries enough water to float the logs, and they all have to come down then. And after that, through the summer, is when we turn last year's dried timbers into this year's lumber. Then of course we stack the lumber to complete the drying. We sell this year what we formed last year, and so on."

"All of which is very interesting, but . . ."

"You weren't paying attention, dear. We've already brought our logs down from the mountain for this season. There won't be anyone working up there again now until early fall. The marking party won't go up until the month you call September."

"So you will hide out up there while I'm down here seeing what Anderson is up to. Hey, that makes sense."

Willie shrugged. "You don't have to stay, you know.

Once you are done killing me, you can collect the rest of your pay and leave. Your part will be done."

"Not on your life," he retorted. "Oh. Excuse me. Bad choice of words under the circumstances. But I mean it. I'll collect the money, no question about that. But I won't leave so soon. You might . . . I don't know . . . you might need me. Or something." He grinned. "Besides, who else would be able to come up and keep you warm at night while you're at that wood-cutting camp? You won't be able to let anyone know but your mother and me. And James. Otherwise people won't act natural about this and Anderson might cotton to the fact that he's being gulled. We wouldn't want it. It'd ruin the whole thing. So if it's all right with you, madame, I prefer to stick around." The grin expanded. "After I kill you."

· 32 ·

Killing Wilhelmina Stout—well, sort of—was remarkably easy. Entirely tragic too, of course. The sad event occurred on the fifth picnic venture they shared. Dexter was devastated. His lamentations were loud and they were many. He drank heavily. He wept bitterly into his brandy and beer. He expressed his sorrow to everyone within hearing. And while he was so vocally and publicly occupied, the "dead" woman's mother performed her motherly duties in order to prepare Wilhelmina for whatever hereafter the Ki'iwa anticipated.

Two days after the "accident" Dex and James entered their favorite saloon, Dex in search of someone new in whom to confide his sorrows and James in search of Rosy, the busty little Ki'iwa whore who'd become so close to his heart of late. Or at any rate close to some portion of his person.

"Where is everybody?" Dex asked.

"The hell with everybody," James corrected. "Where's Rosy?"

The man behind the bar was not Morgan, the usual bartender, but a red-haired stranger. "All the Injuns took off some time before dawn this mornin'. Went up onta th' mounteen. Sons o' bitches woke me up, an' the boss told me t' come fill in over here. Damn if I know what they're doing up there, but far as I can tell there's not a single damn Injun left down here in town. You want somethin' to drink, mister, or are you just gonna jaw?"

"Brandy," Dex said.

"Beer for me." James looked disappointed.

"Is there anybody over at the cafe?" Dex asked. He'd been looking forward to a good meal later.

The redhead shrugged. "I dunno, mister. All I know for sure is what I can see. An' I'm suspicious of half o' that." The man set their drinks down, and James paid for them.

"Today must be the death ceremony the mama told me about," Dex said once the bartender had drifted far enough away that the conversation would not likely be overheard.

"I'd kinda like to see it," James said.

"Whites aren't welcome."

James grinned. "So what's your point, white boy?"

Dex poked him in the ribs. "Asshole. To these people you're just a black white man."

"I'm not sure I like being accused of that." James said.

"That's all right. I don't think it's something you have to worry about happening to you all the time."

"No, I suppose you're right. Once we leave here I'll go back to being another nigger in the woodpile."

"We've both lived in this world the way it really is so far. No point in getting worked up now about how we might like it to be."

"Easier for you to say than me," James said. He lifted his mug and took a long swallow. "One good thing."

"Mmm?"

"This guy knows how to draw a beer without so much head on it."

"See. There are advantages to 'most everything."

"You got plans for the day, Dex?"

He shook his head.

"Since Rosy isn't here I think I'll go out to Anderson's place and see can I get close to that little old Jenny girl that works out there."

"If you run into our erstwhile employer, ask the son of a bitch when he's going to pay us the rest of the fee he agreed to."

"Sure, I can do that little thing. Count on it." James finished his beer, winked at Dexter and ambled off in search of a warm spot to dip his wick into.

Dex took another small sip of his brandy. With the entire town practically empty the day promised to be a dull one.

· 33 ·

There was a note waiting for Dex at the hotel. Inside his room. Lying in plain sight on his bed. The hotel room door had been locked. So much, he thought, for the efficacy of locks.

MEET ME DOWNRIVER, SAME PLACE was all that was on the paper, written in pencil. Each letter was formed in capitals with carefully straight lines and exaggerated curves. No one was going to determine the author by examination of the handwriting, which no doubt was the point of it. There was no signature.

Nor was there need for one. Dex hadn't been downstream along the river except for the lone occasion when he'd spoken with Leroy Anderson.

He considered declining the invitation, at least until James returned from his tomcatting. Dex would have liked to have someone nearby to call on in case there was trouble.

After all, a .45 cartridge costs considerably less than the fifteen hundred dollars Dex was still owed for his successful assassination.

On the other hand, he did want to collect. And besides, this might be an opportunity for him to help Willie Stout by finding out what Anderson was up to.

That, after all, was the purpose behind this charade of her death. And the timing for a meeting with Anderson was good, now while the town was empty of the Ki'iwa.

Dex had no idea how long the tribal ceremonies would run, but Anderson no doubt wanted Dex to show up while the Indians were away at the mountain burial ground.

After only a few moments' hesitation, Dex picked up his hat again and headed downstairs and out into the midday sunlight.

• 34 •

There was only one way to approach the river bend glade where he'd met Anderson's carriage before, and that was by traveling inside the screen of brush that lined the watercourse.

And since there was only one good approach, that was certain to be the place where an ambush would be laid if ambush there was to be.

Dexter ignored the one and only logical route therefore and hiked not out along the creek but first south from the town limits—such as they were—and then out along the open grass where there was no cover except that provided by the slightly rolling terrain and the curvature of the earth itself. From a distance it would not be possible for anyone waiting beside the river to see him, particularly since the river necessarily ran along the lowest course available. His route was much harder on his feet than a direct approach would have been. It was also infinitely safer, a trade-off that he did not mind in the slightest.

He circled far wide of where he thought Anderson should be, then returned to the creek, guided by the tops of the trees he could see in the distance.

He rejoined the creek—river by local reckoning—and

slipped silently upstream until he spotted the carriage precisely where it had been before.

Whatever else Anderson had in mind he obviously intended no shoot-and-run affair. The chunky black cob that brought the carriage here was still in harness, but the horse had been released from between the poles and staked out in the lush grass so it could graze while Anderson waited for Dex—that is, waited for Chance Drewery—to show.

Dex stood for some time leaning against the bole of a large tree, arms crossed and eyes probing, before he decided it was safe to show himself.

Someone, Anderson's segundo Carl he presumed but could not see well enough to be sure of, was standing in a plum thicket upstream from the grassy bend. Whoever it was seemed to be there more as a guard than an ambusher, however, for he made no serious attempt at concealment, simply was posted there where he could keep an eye on things. Dex had no problem with that. It was the sort of precaution he would have expected.

And the carriage was obviously occupied by someone who was becoming more and more restive. The rig lurched heavily from one set of leather springs to the other as a heavy presence inside the box shifted from one side to the other.

Dex waited a little while and then, satisfied there would be no bullet in his back, moved quietly out from cover.

The draft horse saw him coming and pricked its ears but did not whinny or spook. The guard—he could see now that it was indeed Carl—noticed nothing. Dex found it encouraging to note that Carl was armed only with a belt gun. If quick mayhem were intended, he felt sure a rifle or shotgun would have been employed.

Dex nonetheless took the small precaution of placing the body of the carriage between himself and Carl before he crept up to the carriage door and in a soft voice announced, "I'm here."

It pleased him to note that he'd managed to reach the rig quite undetected. He was sure of that from Anderson's reaction. From inside the closed carriage he heard a sharp, gasping little cry and the body of the coach rocked wildly when the fat man leaped in fright.

"Don't *do* that," Anderson complained.

"Open the door," Dex said.

"It isn't locked."

"Open it anyway, please. And I'd prefer it if you keep both hands in view when you do."

"Oh, I . . . I understand. Sorry."

The carriage rocked again, leaning toward Dex this time, and a moment later the door swung open.

Anderson was alone on the backseat. He had both hands held out—empty—for Dex to see. He must have been waiting there for quite some time, Dex thought, because his shirt was sodden with sweat, and a damp handkerchief was draped over one knee.

"Are you armed?"

"No," Anderson told him. It might or might not have been true.

Dex glanced back toward the town. Carl was still standing there just inside the screen of brush, still unaware that Dex had arrived. Dex was quite willing for the man to remain in that state of ignorance. He looked behind him also, certain he hadn't been followed from town but wanting to take a look anyway, then climbed inside the carriage with Anderson and pulled the door quietly closed behind him.

· 35 ·

"You're as good as your reputation suggested," Anderson said with a grunt of satisfaction.

"Thank you." Dex inclined his head in modest acknowledgment of the compliment. It did occur to him, though, to realize with something of a chill that living up to Chance Drewery's reputation was not altogether a good thing. After all, if the man really was such an exceptionally skilled assassin . . . and if he did happen to finally show up in Ki'iwa . . .

Anderson leaned forward, having to strain against an immense bulge of belly in order to do so, and fetched a leather valise off the floor. He placed it onto his knee—a man of ordinary proportion might have chosen to set it onto his lap, but Anderson's was already fully occupied with rolls of fat—and unbuckled the clasps.

Dex offered no warnings. But he did rest his hand rather conspicuously on the grip of the Webley revolver on his belt.

Anderson saw and said, "If there is anything I do not want or need, sir, it would be to offer offense to a man of your . . . um . . . particular talents."

Dex grunted. And left his hand where it was.

The fat man drew a leather pouch from the valise and laid it onto the seat at his side, carefully closed the valise and returned it to the floor. Then he handed the pouch to Dexter.

"Heavy," Dex observed.

"Yes, I, uh, want to speak with you about that."

"Go right ahead."

"I owe you fifteen hundred for the successful completion of your, um, work here."

"That's right."

"The full amount is in there. Plus a bonus of five hundred. No one has questioned the accidental nature of Mrs. Stout's . . . shall we say . . . unfortunate demise."

"It's what you asked for."

"Exactly." Anderson picked up his handkerchief and mopped his face with it although the cloth was already so wet Dex didn't see that it could do much more than rearrange the sweat. "I included another five hundred on top of that."

Dex raised an eyebrow.

"I will have more work for you in the near future," the fat man said.

"Is that right?" Goodness but this was one murderous S.O.B., Dex was thinking. Now that he'd gotten a taste for mayhem on demand he apparently was finding it useful. And perhaps enjoyable as well.

"A man this time though. I believe your fee for an ordinary, uh, piece of work is one thousand? Half now and the remainder upon completion. Just like, um, the first job?"

"An accident again?"

"It would be nice. It will not be strictly necessary this time."

"Two thousand," Dex said. What the hell. When the dice are hot, roll them.

"I thought the usual was . . ."

"Two thousand. Take it or leave it." Dex kept his voice cold and disinterested although his heart was thumping at a furious rate. Negotiating a murder for hire was not something he had much prior experience with, the real Drewery having established the terms for Wilhelmina Stout's killing.

Anderson did not appear to be particularly troubled by the demand. He nodded. "All right then. Two thousand."

"The five hundred in hand can be considered expense money. Have your man Carl deliver the one thousand down payment at your earliest convenience, if you please."

Anderson wiped his face again. "Yes. All right."

"Who am I supposed to kill?"

"I . . . I'll give you the name soon. In a week or so. Then you can, uh, complete your work and . . . leave. I trust you . . . they say you have high standards. They say a man is never . . ." He ran out of words. And nerve. The sweat was running down his neck now, soaking into his collar. Linen collars were a poor choice for Leroy Anderson, Dex thought. The man really should buy the patent celluloid collars. They stand up ever so much better to moisture and soiling, after all.

"Is blackmail the term you're looking for?" Dex asked mildly.

"I wouldn't have . . . that is to say . . ."

"You'll not hear from me again once I've received final payment," Dex assured him.

"Yes, I . . . thank you. Thank you." Anderson mopped his face, his discomfort obvious. If Dex had had a hand-kerchief in his pocket he would have offered it, if only so the fat man's chins wouldn't *glisten* so. It was disconcerting to say the least. Disgusting too. They gleamed in a ray of light peeking in past the carriage side curtain and high-lighted the nervous trembling of the soft, gelatinous flesh.

"Is there anything else?" Dex stifled an impulse to in-quire whether the man wanted trophies this time. Ears, per-haps. Or a scalp. This was Indian country, after all. A scalp might be a rather nice addition to the wall in the gentle-man's study.

"No, I shall have Carl bring you the thousand tonight."

"Very well."

"And . . . Mr. Drewery . . ."

"Yes?"

"You really have been a big help to me. Thank you."

"Any time." "Nice doing business with you." "Always a pleasure to serve and to satisfy." Would one of those commercial sentiments be appropriate under these circumstances? Dex decided—reluctantly—that sarcasm would not do here. Instead he only grunted and, taking the blood money with him, left the carriage as silently and as stealthily as he'd come.

Carl, he was fairly sure, never had an inkling that the man he was guarding already received the visit.

♦ 36 ♦

"Jesus," James blurted when he saw all the money scattered atop the blanket on Dex's bed.

"I wish there was a bank in town," Dex commented after filling James in on their current state of impending employment.

"Why's that?"

"All this coin looks mighty nice . . . and it is . . . but it'd sure be easier if we could convert it to currency. Gold weighs s' damn much."

James looked at his old friend and shook his head in a display of deep sorrow. "Dex boy, I do worry about you. Any man who'd complain because he has too much gold to carry . . ."

Dex brightened. "You're right. I'll shut up. Especially since you're the one who's gonna be doing the carrying."

James gave the jumble of beautifully minted coins a more critical inspection. "First bank we come to . . ."

"Exactly. Now tell me how your day has been. You know about mine. How'd you make out at the Anderson ranch?"

James rolled his eyes and let out a soft whistle. "Jenny isn't bad, I'm telling you. Of course she doesn't have tits to match Rosy's. Those melons Rosy carries around on her chest are 'most enough to make a poor boy fall in love. Jenny can't match those. But she's a nice girl despite that. Plump. Good thing is, I happen to like them plump, with enough meat on the bones to grab hold of when things get busy."

"Quit bragging and get to the point."

"Jenny's an Indian," James insisted on adding. "First girl I was ever with that wasn't colored. Besides Rosy, that is."

"Was it any different?"

"No. I'd sort of thought it would be, but the truth is it wasn't. Not that I'm complaining."

Dex frowned. "If the girl is Indian, why wasn't she at the burial ceremony for Willie?"

"Because she isn't Ki'iwa, that's why. She's Delaware."

"From all the way back east?"

James shrugged. "All I know is she said her tribe is Delaware. Considering what-all she was doing while she was talking it never occurred to me to press her for particulars."

"Let's skip over that part of it, shall we? Did you find out anything worth knowing?"

"Maybe. I'm not sure. I mean, it isn't like our boy Leroy confides in her. Although I did learn a bit about the man's personal habits. Not that I can think of any reason why we'd care."

"We can get into that later if we need to. What about Willie and Anderson wanting her dead?"

"Nothing direct, of course. That isn't the sort of thing he'd talk to Jenny about. But I did encourage her to talk and asked as many questions as I thought I could get away with without it being obvious that I was grilling her."

Dex nodded.

"I know Anderson has been visited three different times this past year by a fancy-dressed gent and that Leroy got excited and eager about something each time the man came. Jenny said the visitor's name was Sinclair. Olin Sinclair. And he must be really important because Anderson loaned her to him overnight each time he visited, and he's never done that with any other guest. So she's sure he isn't a cattle buyer or salesman of some sort. He's much more important than that. She thinks . . . she isn't sure, mind, but she thinks he has something to do with a railroad."

"That doesn't make much sense. There isn't a railroad anywhere near here."

"Maybe not," James said. "But just because there isn't one now, that doesn't mean there couldn't be one someday. Maybe even someday soon."

It was Dex's turn to whistle. "And if one is built through this part of the country, could be that Mr. Leroy H. Anderson intends to profit from it. At the expense of the Ki'iwa tribe perhaps?"

"That's kinda what I got to thinking too," James said.

Dex frowned. "Except for one thing."

"Mmm?"

"The Railroad Act. I didn't pay all that much attention to it, but if I remember right, the government will give railroad builders land as a premium for them building the road. It gives whatever right of way they need plus alternating sections on either side of the right of way. If the government is doing that, there wouldn't be any reason for Anderson and this Sinclair fellow to try and come up with a land scheme. The railroad, if there's to be one, would already have whatever land they need. After all, the federal government already owns the reservation land. I expect they could give it away and . . . I don't know . . . move the Ki'iwa someplace else or maybe squeeze them onto smaller reservation holdings if that's what they want."

"Maybe it isn't land that's needed," James suggested.

"Then what?"

James could only shake his head. "Damned if I know. But there has to be some mighty good reason for Anderson to spend this much money just to have a widow lady killed."

"Widow lady and President of the tribal council. Don't forget that little detail."

"I still don't see the reason for the murder," James told him. "But we both know there has to be one. And it isn't anger. According to Jenny, Wilhelmina Stout has never visited at the ranch, and Jenny's never once heard the lady's name mentioned. Not even these past few days. Anderson acts like she doesn't exist . . . which come to think of it he thinks is so . . . but then he never said anything about her when he thought she was alive either."

"What does he talk about?"

"Sex mostly. The man's too damn fat to fuck properly, but Jenny says he's horny as a pair of billygoats. She has to blow him first thing each morning and again before he goes to sleep at night." James made a sour face. "And I want to tell you, I paid dearly for that bit of information. I'd already been kissing her before she got around to telling me that."

"Next time you go out there, take her a poke of mints to freshen her breath."

"Yeah. Thanks," James said dryly.

"Did she say the man talks about anything that could be of any possible interest to us?"

"Cows. She said he talks to his riding hands about cows. Talks to cattle buyers a couple times a year. The only other thing I learned about him is that he's been getting mail pretty regularly for the past six months from Pennsylvania State College."

"He's an alumnus?" Dex suggested.

James shook his head. "I assumed that too, but Jenny says Anderson boasts sometimes about being a self-made man. That he never went past eighth grade in school and is proud of it."

"Penn State, huh."

"That's what she said."

"She doesn't know what the mail is?"

"Some newsletter sort of thing, but she's never read one. Actually I don't think the girl knows how to read. She only knows these newsletters are from the college because of overhearing Anderson say something about them to Sinclair the last time the man visited."

"And when was that?"

"Two months ago."

"Not long before Anderson contracted with Chance Drewery for the murder."

"You'd think there would be a connection," James agreed. "But what?"

"It might help if we knew more about those newsletters."

"I'll see what I can do," James said.

"Good. And in the meantime see if you can think of someplace we can hide all this gold. It kinda makes me nervous having it lying around in the room like this. Especially since Carl already knows where we are and how to come in whenever he wants."

"There should be a safe downstairs. That would do until we're ready to leave."

"Good idea. We'll ask about that as soon as Eugene Duckwing gets back from the ceremony." Dex grinned. "And don't forget, we're to have another thousand to add to the kitty. He said he'd have Carl deliver it this evening."

"I'm glad we came here," James said. Then he sobered. "I think."

◆ 37 ◆

James cocked his head to one side and held a finger up to ask for silence. He was obviously listening to or for something although Dex had no idea what it was that alerted him.

James listened for only a few moments, then whispered, "Back stairs. Somebody's trying to come up real quiet."

"Anderson's man Carl?" Dex suggested.

"Maybe so, maybe no."

Dex reacted immediately, without taking time to ponder the possibilities. Most of the likely reasons were entirely innocent and benign. But not all of them. He pointed to the floor beside James's bed.

The two friends had been together too many years to need verbal communication on some things. James nodded and reached for his brace of .32 caliber revolvers. Dex glanced toward the door. When he looked back toward the bed there was no sign of James there. But the blanket that covered his bed had been pulled askew so that it now hung down to floor level on that side of the hotel bed.

Dex waited and after a few minutes saw the doorknob silently turn. No one knocked to request entry. No one

came inside either. James had locked the door when he
came in earlier.

Curious, Dex remained where he was. He did, however,
slip the big Webley from its holster and lay it next to his
thigh, with his hand resting not so casually on the grips.

He heard a faint scrape of metal on metal as someone
very expertly picked the door lock. The knob rattled
slightly and this time turned far enough to release the latch.

When Carl stepped unannounced into Dex's room he
found himself peering straight into the muzzle of the Webley. Dex's aim centered high on the bridge of the lean
man's nose. It was a sight that was bound to be unnerving.
Carl blinked and looked, well, unnerved.

He twitched just a little and then politely said, "I didn't
know there was anybody in here. I'm . . . sorry." He
sounded like those last couple words came mighty hard to
his tongue.

Dex grunted and returned the Webley to the bed at his
side.

"I brought your money."

Dex nodded.

"It's . . . you won't mind if I reach into my pocket?"

"Feel free." Dex smiled. And laid his hand onto the grips
of the Webley again.

Carl dug deep into his right-hand pocket and produced a
rather small coin purse. But then how big does a purse have
to be to hold fifty coins no larger than a silver quarter
dollar. "It's all here."

"I'm sure it is," Dex told him.

Carl tossed the purse onto the bed. Dex allowed it to
drop and made no move to pick it up.

"You can count it if you want."

"No need for that. I doubt that Mr. Anderson would like
it if you filched some of my money."

Carl's face colored a rather rich reddish hue at the suggestion. But he did not say anything about that. Instead he
licked his lips and hesitated for a moment, then said, "You
didn't have to go and do what you done today. Mr. Anderson didn't like that, and that's a fact."

"Didn't like something I did?" Dex asked. "Or something you didn't do?"

"You know what I mean, dammit. You snuck in without me seeing. Mr. Anderson was real pissed off about that."

"With you," Dex noted, "not me."

"Well yeah, but . . ."

"How did I know you weren't laying ready to put a bullet in my back."

"I wasn't," Carl protested.

"This time," Dex agreed. "But maybe that's only because Anderson has more work for me. Next time, Carl, you wait out in plain sight. You hear? Next time I come past you I won't leave you standing there and you won't be a threat to me or anybody else. You understand what I'm telling you?"

Carl turned from angry red to frightened pale in little more than a heartbeat. "You . . . came down through the fucking *woods*, man?"

Dex didn't say anything. Which, technically speaking, meant that he told no lie. Of course if Carl wanted to believe that Dex—or rather, Chance Drewery—was so damned good that he was able to slip through the woods and past Carl's nose undetected, well, Dex saw no harm in the man making such an assumption. He was, in fact, quite welcome to do so.

A thin sheen of sweat—cold, no doubt—began to show on the man's forehead. Maybe it had something to do with his long association with Sweatin' Leroy Anderson, Dex surmised. Or not. Dex managed to stifle an impulse toward a smug smile. That would go past intimidation and on into the realm of mocking insult. Sensible folk, particularly those who do not have the same skills as a real assassin might, are better off to refrain from waving red flags under bulls' noses. Particularly when those bulls carry large-caliber revolving pistols.

"Was there anything else you wanted to see me about?" Dex asked.

Carl shook his head.

"Drop by any time," Dex offered. "But next time you

might remember to knock before you enter."

"Yes, sir."

Dex considered it a genuine victory to hear that little ol' three-letter word "sir" come out of Carl's mouth.

"And remember. If Mr. Anderson ever has business with me again, you'd be wise to post yourself right alongside that carriage. I don't mind a man doing his job and defending his employer. In fact I wouldn't respect you if you didn't. But I don't want there to be any reason why you and I should get crossways with each other. All right?"

"Yes." Carl licked his lips again. "Sir." It seemed to come easier to him this time.

Dex nodded and gave the man a friendly smile. "Thank you for bringing this by," he said. "If you're in the saloon later on this evening I'd be pleased to buy you a drink."

"Thank you. Sir."

"Good night, Carl."

"Good night, sir."

· 38 ·

The Ki'iwa remained on the mountain doing whatever it was that they did for a full three days.

James had the companionship of Anderson's cook cum housekeeper Jenny to help him through the wait. Dexter had a pile of gold coins to watch over. The coins, he found, were damn small comfort. By the time Eugene Duckwing showed up behind the hotel desk, acting as if he hadn't been away for longer than to take a coffee break, Dex was so horny he was afraid he would start to honk.

He was becoming damn-all hungry too, for the few places in town where one could find a meal were all shuttered and silent save for the saloons. And after several days free lunches had begun to seem mighty expensive to him. He would gladly have swapped a considerable amount of gold for one really good home-cooked meal like James's mother used to prepare. The thought of one more pickled egg or another chunk of fly-specked ham was just about more than he could stomach.

James, damn him, compounded the problem by relating in excruciating detail every morsel and mouthful that Jenny prepared for him during his daily jaunts out to the Anderson ranch.

"Where are you going?" James asked after breakfast—breakfast! A real one: bacon and hotcakes and hominy enough to fill a bucket . . . or a very hungry Dexter Yancey—the morning the Ki'iwa returned.

Dex just grinned at him and winked. He pointed to the poke where they'd stashed their pay. "Get Eugene to do something with that, will you? Me, I'm gonna go for a little ride."

"Enjoy yourself."

"Oh, I expect to. I surely do. Look for me back in . . . I dunno . . . two or three days."

"And if Anderson's man comes around looking for you?"

"Tell him I'll be back by and by."

"Yeah, well, tell the lady hello from me, will you?"

"James, I doubt your name will come up for at least the first forty-eight hours. I mean, I don't know how to tell you this, but I just don't expect to be wasting time thinking about some ugly colored boy. Not when that pretty li'l Indian maid is around."

"Maid?"

Dex shrugged. And grinned. "Close enough for my purposes. And better yet, far enough away from maidenhood to make the ride up there worthwhile. Tell you what, though. While I'm gone, why don't you try again to convince Jenny to swipe one of those Penn State newsletters."

"She's scared, Dex. She's afraid of what might happen if she's caught and Anderson gets mad at her. Son of a bitch has a mean temper, she tells me."

"You can talk her into it."

"I don't know that I want to, actually. She's a nice girl. I don't want to frighten her."

"We need a look at one of those papers, James."

"Maybe. Maybe not. They could have nothing to do with any of this."

"Which we won't really know until we see one," Dex pointed out.

James sighed. "I'll see what I can do."

"Nobody can ask better than that." Dex tugged his hat

snug, winked at James and stepped out of the hotel room feeling like a brand-new man now that the Ki'iwa were back off the mountain . . . and Willie was alone up there in her hiding place.

◆ 39 ◆

Dex gasped and wriggled. He pulled half away from Wilhelmina's touch. But only half. He did not want it to stop. But the feel of her tongue was so intense he practically cried out. This was pleasure so fierce it was close to being pain.

Dex quite truly hadn't known that a man's nipple could be as sensitive as this, but Willie's prolonged attentions—sucking, licking, sometimes even lightly nipping with her teeth—had aroused him beyond his ability to judge the thin line that separated pain from pleasure.

He loved what she was doing. But he just couldn't take much more of it without something bursting.

As much as an excuse to change position as anything else, he grabbed the girl around the waist and pulled her to him, positioning her on her side so that the dark, smooth bush of her pelvic hair was tickling his nose and so that his pulsing, aching, *far* more than merely ready cock was nudging her chin.

Willie laughed, perhaps understanding the reason for this demand, and took Dex into her mouth.

When he reciprocated with the tentative probing of his

tongue across her most sensitive flesh the girl began to whimper and writhe.

Dex avoided the moist depths between her labia and concentrated instead on the tiny button of pleasure that lay at the top of her slit. Wilhelmina obviously approved of the choice. He could feel her passions rise, could feel the onset of a deep-rooted pulsing inside her body, could feel the burst of pleasure surge through her when she reached a quick climax.

Willie cried out, stiffening momentarily, then returned with renewed vigor to the task of milking Dex's juices from his loins into her eager mouth.

It was a task that took only minutes. But then they'd both been kissing, licking, touching and tasting for the past hour or so.

Dex shuddered as the hot fluid pumped and flowed from him, and Willie obliged by wrapping her lips tight around him and greedily swallowing everything he had to offer.

Later, when he was depleted and she could suck no final drops out of him, she sighed and sat upright to lean over him and stroke his cheeks and forehead.

"If I'd known white men were this good," she said, "I would have been begging passing strangers for a tumble as soon as I started my periods."

"Oh, they're not all as good as I am," Dex assured her with a straight face. "The fact is you just got lucky when you found me. I'm much better than most men of any color."

"That explains it then," Willie said, her voice and expression every bit as solemn as his had been.

She bent down and kissed him. When she sat up again she made a sour face. "You taste like fish," she complained.

"Funny. I thought it was you. You tasted sort of salty, I thought."

"Maybe we're kissing the wrong parts then."

"Want to go again?" he offered.

"Give me a few minutes to recover, will you? My heart has hardly slowed down since this last one."

"Ten minutes. No more," he told her.

"That sounds all right." She bent down again and this time lightly kissed the tip of his cock. "Mmm," she said. "Tasty."

"So are you."

"Seriously. Do you think so? It isn't . . . nasty? Or anything?"

"Of course not. It's clean and pleasant."

"Not fishy?"

He laughed. "I've heard women say that before, but I don't have any idea where the notion came from. Personally, I don't like the taste of fish. But I sure do enjoy the flavor of a nice clean pussy."

"Are you sure all white men aren't this good?" she asked. "Or are you just trying to avoid competition."

"I have no competition. Hadn't you noticed?"

"Yes. And you're modest too."

"It is one of my more notable attributes, it's true," Dex said modestly. Willie laughed.

"Is ten minutes up yet?" she asked. A good thirty or forty seconds must have gone by since they'd agreed to the rest period.

"At least that long," Dex said.

"Could have been more," the Ki'iwa girl agreed.

"Come here, please." Dex reached up. Took her into his arms. Felt the immediate stirrings of desire begin to swell insistently.

This beat hell out of sitting in a hotel room with a bunch of gold, he decided as Willie's tongue probed beyond his teeth.

· 40 ·

Dex heard a soft, droning, rather sonorous sound away in the distance somewhere. It took him a moment to identify. It was a snore. More to the point, it was himself. Snoring. Very lightly but . . . be damned. He must have drifted off for a minute or so there. And he must have been very, very deeply satisfied to have arrived at so complete a state of relaxation as all that. Well, he'd come by it honestly enough. And pleasantly.

As he returned from that soft and distance place he became aware of Willie's hand cupping his balls and the weight of her pretty head on his shoulder. He could feel her breath slow and easy on his skin. He tried to avoid moving lest he waken her. Then she spoke and he discovered he was not the one who'd needed that precaution.

"Welcome back," she said, her voice melodious and low. She chuckled a little and very gently squeezed his cods by way of a greeting.

"Was I asleep very long?"

"Not very."

He allowed his head to roll to one side and kissed her. This was one thoroughly likable girl, he was discovering.

"Are you hungry?"

"Um hmm."

"Get up then. I'll fix us something for supper."

"I didn't bring much," he said. "I didn't want to arouse suspicions." He'd put what was left from his and James's traveling rations into his saddlebags but the only shopping he'd done to prepare for coming up the mountain was to buy a pint bottle of brandy.

"I already have everything I need," Willie told him.

"Your mother supplied you?"

"Yes," she said. "My mother the earth."

Dex didn't entirely understand that until Wilhelmina began assembling their supper. She had trout fresh from the stream and more trout that had been smoked and dried.

"Tastes like pussy," she told him with a smile as she gutted a fresh fish and dropped it head, skin and all into a skillet of hot grease.

She had some sort of greens that he was fairly sure he may have seen before but certainly never noticed nor would have thought of as a food.

There were wild mushrooms, an assortment of berries and a roasted root that was a mystery to him. It all, however, tasted fine when it came time to surround the meal.

"I thought you Ki'iwa were civilized," he said as he helped himself to another pile of mushrooms and greens. There was plenty of fish left too, but even though Willie was without question a fine cook Dex would much rather eat pussy than trout.

"We are. Have been for generations. But we haven't forgotten everything our grandfathers learned." She gave a haughty sniff and helped herself to another of the fresh trout that Dex spurned. "Would you like more of the fried termites?"

Dex wasn't sure what his expression looked like, but whatever it was it drew a hearty laugh from Wilhelmina. "That isn't . . . I mean, not *really* . . . ?"

She laughed. But did not otherwise answer, leaving him uncertain whether he'd just been eating—and, worse, enjoying—cooked insects . . . or if the girl was merely pulling his leg. He hoped to hell she was teasing.

"So tell me," she said around a mouthful of fish, "what is happening back home?"

Dex filled her in with all they'd learned. Not that there was so very much to tell.

"Another murder?" Willie's eyes were wide and she shuddered. "Who?"

"He said he'd know in a week or so. He won't tell me until then."

"But he wants another person killed?"

Dex shrugged. "He's sure enough about it to've given me a down payment on my fee. And it's important enough to him that he didn't quibble when I told him I wanted more than my . . . or rather this Drewery fellow's . . . usual thousand dollars."

"I suppose I should feel flattered that I was worth three thousand to him if one is normal. Funny thing. It doesn't make me feel any better about it."

"If it makes any difference, ma'am, I wouldn't *really* kill you for less than, oh, six or seven thousand."

Willie made a face and threw a trout skeleton at him. The bones hit him in the chest and slid into his lap, leaving a smear of grease behind.

"Could we be serious for a minute here please?" she asked.

"You're the one trying to start a food fight, not me."

"Is it to be another member of the tribe you're to kill?" she asked.

Dex could only shrug. "Anderson didn't say. Could be he's expecting a visitor that he wants out of the way or . . . I don't know. For that matter, I don't know very much at all about any of this. It's all confusing to me. That reminds me, though. Do you know a man named Olin Sinclair?"

Willie thought for a moment, then shook her head. Dex explained where he'd heard the name.

"No, I'm sure I've never met him. Nor heard about him, for that matter."

"What about Pennsylvania State College? Did your husband have any dealings with them that you know about?"

"No, never. At least not that I know of. It's a school, I presume?"

Dex nodded.

Willie shook her head again. "I never heard of it before this moment," she said, "and I doubt George did either. Certainly he never said anything to me about any schools. In Pennsylvania or anywhere else."

Dex grunted. He would have enjoyed another helping of the mushrooms. But if there were termites cooked in with the mushrooms . . .

"Does that have something to do with Anderson's plan? Whatever that is?"

"I don't know for sure. This Sinclair fellow has visited several times in the past year according to Anderson's housemaid, and lately Anderson has been receiving a newsletter of some kind from Penn State. But we don't know if there is any significance to either of those things. They could be unrelated."

"How are you learning all this?"

Dex explained.

"I know Jenny, of course. She's a Delaware. Delawares lie, you know."

"I didn't know that."

"Oh, yes. Delawares are bad for lying."

"May be," Dex said, "but James tells me she gives a great blow job."

Willie sniffed disdainfully. "I'm sure she isn't anything like as good as I am."

"You may have to prove that," Dex challenged.

"I thought I already did."

"Yeah, but I have a terrible memory. It needs to be refreshed from time to time."

"I can do that," Willie said quite cheerfully.

Later, considerably later, the widow Wilhelmina Stout sighed and wistfully said, "I miss my home, Dexter. And I'm kind of scared too. If Mr. Anderson finds out I'm still alive . . . and up here . . ."

"He'd have to come through me first, dear. Him and any son of a bitch he pays to come after you."

"You're sweet," Willie said.

Dex liked the idea that she thought so. Liked it so much that he decided against mentioning to her that fighting and gunplay and nonsense like that were really not his particular cup of tea, that he would much rather talk his way out of trouble than resort to the gun or the blade.

Still, he really did like this lovely girl. And he really would defend her to the best of his ability.

· 41 ·

"What? You got lost and just now found your way back? Next time keep one thing in mind. The town is on the flat ground. To get back here you go downhill. Even you should be able to manage that, white boy."

Dex wadded up the dirty shirt he'd just removed and threw it. The balled cloth came open in flight and fluttered harmlessly to the floor at James's feet. He didn't even have to duck to avoid it.

Dex had been gone three days. He hadn't intended to remain on the mountain anywhere near that long. But then once he was up there he'd found it difficult to tell Wilhelmina good-bye again.

At least he wasn't horny any longer. Well, not as badly so anyway. It had taken some hours to ride down from the logging camp this morning, and a nooner would have been nice.

"Are you hungry?" James asked.

"Damn right." And for something other than fish. Willie had a shotgun with her but did not want to fire it to bring down game for fear someone might hear and come see what the noise was about.

"The special at the cafe today is pot roast," James offered.

"I'd kill for a pot roast right now," Dex declared.

"That's sad," James told him. "Just a couple days ago you swore you wouldn't do it for less than two thousand. My oh my, how your standards have fallen."

Dex changed quickly into clean clothing, bundled the things he'd been wearing—or frequently not wearing—for the past three days together ready to be laundered and picked up his cane. He'd left it behind when he rode up to visit with Willie and had rather missed it. Not that he needed it, but carrying the cane was both a habit and an affectation. And the presence of a slim sword blade inside the hollowed out malacca shaft was comforting even if old-fashioned.

"Ready when you are, darky."

James gave him an exaggerated flash of teeth, white against the chocolate hue of his skin, and said, "Yowzuh, bossman, yowzuh."

"Asshole," Dex accused.

James only grinned at him. The real thing this time. Then led the way out into the second floor corridor.

"You embarrass me sometimes, you know that?" James said.

"I'd be embarrassed too if I were as homely as you and traveling in the company of a handsome, well set-up gentleman such as myself."

"Do you realize that is your third helping of pot roast?"

"Aw, who's counting?"

"I am for one. So's that guy over there."

"Bullshit."

"No, Dexter, you're causing a scene. You're really very embarrassing."

Dex would have ordered another serving of the tender beef if only he thought he could hold it without causing his gut to burst. As it was he'd had to move his belt buckle over a notch. But he'd thought he got away with it without anyone noticing.

James was only woofing him, of course. Dex knew that. But he couldn't help glancing in the direction James indicated when he claimed people were staring.

There were three other tables occupied in the cafe at the moment, and the gentlemen at two of them seemed entirely unaware of Dex and James in the corner.

A lone man at the third table, though, did indeed seem to be sending surreptitious looks their way.

The fellow was obviously a man of some breeding and taste. He wore a carefully tailored broadcloth suit, batwing collar and carefully knotted tie with what looked like a diamond stickpin—and no tiny chip it was either—winking at the center of the knot.

He had on a cream-colored vest with spats to match, a heavy gold chain across his belly and an ornate fob that probably represented one of the fraternal orders. Dex did not recognize it, but then he'd never been much interested in secret societies. They'd always struck him as being more comical than serious albeit unintentionally so. This gent obviously did not agree.

The fellow was perhaps fifty years old and was going to gray. He had fluffy Burnside whiskers and hooded, exceptionally pale eyes. On the chair at his side lay a pair of soft leather gloves almost the same cream shade as his vest and spats, and a cane with a bulbous gold head.

The looks he kept giving to Dex and James were . . . odd. Dex couldn't quite decide if the man was simply awed by his appetite—unlikely though that was; a proper gentleman such as this man appeared to be would not wish to give offense with any outward displays of unwonted interest—or if there might be some other unfathomable reason for his attention. But attention and awareness there were, never mind that the fellow was trying to be unobtrusive about it.

Dex hadn't noticed it himself, his own attention being riveted on the novelty of having real food on the plate before him, but James had.

Of a sudden Dex felt an impulse—no, something stronger than mere impulse; a definite, insistent urge—to leave the cafe.

He dropped his napkin on top of his plate and without waiting for the dried apple pie that the chalkboard said came with each dinner said, "Pay for us here, would you, buddy?"

He walked quickly out onto the street, leaving James to settle up for the kitchen wreckage Dex's hunger may have caused.

· 42 ·

"Will you be needing anything, Mr. Milton?"

"Not that I think of at the moment, Mr. Duckwing."

"If you don't mind a suggestion, sir, you might want to dine early this evening."

The idea was not especially appealing. Not after such a huge lunch. "Why is that, Mr. Duckwing?"

"Tribal meeting tonight, sir. Nearly everything in town will be closed down, just like it was during the ceremonial for Mrs. Stout. Tonight we have to choose the new council president. Everyone is supposed to be there. And sir."

"Yes?"

"Please pass the message along to Mr. Emory in case I don't see him."

"Of course, Eugene. And thank you for warning us." James had gone out to the Anderson place to court Jenny. Or whatever.

"My pleasure, sir," Duckwing said. "You and Mr. Emory are valued customers."

Dex smiled. "Also your only customers."

"Oh, no sir. Another gentleman checked in just yester-day." Duckwing permitted himself an answering smile. "I'll try to bear up under the strain of the crowd though, never fear."

"I have every confidence in you, Mr. Duckwing," Dex said with a chuckle as he headed for the stairs.

"Dammit," Dex mumbled a few moments later when he entered his room. There was another note there. On the bed. The room had been entered and the message dropped off while they were at lunch. Dex thought he'd cured Carl of that. Obviously he was mistaken in that belief.

AFTER DARK TONIGHT. SAME PLACE. BE THERE.

It wasn't signed. But then it didn't have to be.

Anderson had made up his mind about the next contract killing, Dex supposed, and now either wanted to give him the name or reclaim his down payment. Fat chance.

Dex found himself quite honestly hoping that the killing was still wanted though. Not that he was feeling particularly malicious toward anyone in or around Ki'iwa. But having work here—such as it was—gave him an excuse to remain in the town.

And he did want to be of help to Willie Stout. He had no idea how he could best do that. But he wanted to be ready if or when the time came.

Dex dipped into his vest pocket and fetched his watch out. It was barely the middle of the afternoon. With any kind of luck James would be back before Dex had to leave to make the rendezvous with the fat man.

Not that Dexter expected any danger tonight. But he just plain felt better when he knew James was behind him . . . and knew too that the other parties were not aware of that fact.

• 43 •

Nightfall came. James didn't. The note said after dark, but it did not say exactly when. Screw 'em.

Eventually though, when it was approaching ten o'clock, Dex conceded that probably James would not be returning to the hotel. Dammit. He would have been happier with James there to back him up.

On the other hand, he'd met with Anderson twice now. And Carl seemed pretty thoroughly cowed, despite the man's sneaking in again to leave this latest message. After all, it wasn't the sort of note one would like to post on the outside of the door for passing strangers to read, particularly now that there was indeed a stranger in the hotel who might pass by.

Dex got himself ready and went outside. There was no sign of Eugene Duckwing in the lobby, and the town was silent and dark. Dex had no idea where the tribal meeting was being held, but it sure wasn't happening anywhere close by. That many people would surely make some noise, and on a still night like this noise would carry far.

The first time Dex met Anderson he followed Carl through the creek-side brush. The second time he'd circled wide and came up from the downstream side. This time, not to break the trend of being unpredictable, he decided to walk in plain sight across the plain. He wouldn't creep up on anyone that way. But neither would anyone else be able to hide in unseen ambush.

In that regard he was glad now that he'd waited so long for James's never-happened arrival. A three-quarter moon had risen well clear of the horizon and the expanse of open grass was lighted with a thin but exceptionally bright silver-tinged light.

There would be deep shadows inside the line of dense growth along the creek—river, if they wished—but there was moonlight enough that even beneath the thin canopy of the trees on the flat that Anderson favored Dex should be able to see fairly well.

Dex stayed well away from the creek and marched quickly parallel to it, then swung left toward the break in the tree line that marked the river bend where he knew the carriage would be.

Except this time there was no carriage parked on the swath of lush, sweet smelling grass.

This time Dex saw a horse standing tied there and a solitary figure in dark silhouette beneath the trees.

The man looked too thick-bodied to be Carl but much, much too thin to be Leroy Anderson.

Besides, Dex doubted there was a horse alive that could carry Anderson's weight on its back.

Whoever this was . . .

Dex's first impulse was to turn and march right the hell back to town.

On the other hand, he was close to the grove before he ever noticed the man in the shadows. By now the man surely saw him. To turn and walk away like that would have seemed cowardly. Particularly so when there seemed to be no threat presented. The fellow was standing in full view. He seemed calm and relaxed, and he held no weapon.

Dex grimaced, feeling a small flutter of concern deep in his belly.

But he continued on toward the grove, altering neither his path nor his gait.

He had, however, been known to do other stupid things in the past.

◆ 44 ◆

"Good evening." The man moved slightly when he spoke, and Dex felt a cold chill of alarm. He held something in his left hand. An object that he'd had tucked close beside his leg.

Then Dex saw what the article was and felt a sense of relief. It was only a cane.

Dex was close then, within a matter of yards, able to better see. This, he was fairly sure, was the same gentleman who'd been in the cafe at lunchtime.

He'd been paying close attention to Dex and James then. Had he seen or presumed something that prompted this meeting?

Except no, that made no sense. Dex found the note when he returned to the hotel immediately following lunch. The message had to have been placed in his room while he and James were in the cafe. And they'd left there before this gentleman.

Dex decided not to worry about it. Whatever this concerned, he would surely find out now.

"Yes," he responded to the gentleman's greeting. "Good evening to you too, sir."

"You are Mr. Drewery, I believe?" the man said.

"You are mistaken, sir. My name is John Milton."

"So it says in the register," the gent agreed. He laughed softly. "I must tell you that I enjoy your poetry. But you are a younger man than I expect."

"Another John Milton, obviously," Dex answered. "But I have to agree with you about his writings. And you would be . . . ?"

The gentleman hesitated a few seconds. Then said, "My name is Drewery. Chance Drewery."

Dex felt the bottom drop out of his stomach.

He should have turned around and headed back to town when he had the chance.

He should have waited for James.

He should have stayed the fuck down in Texas.

For that matter, he never should have left home.

He should have . . .

"It's a pleasure to meet you," he heard himself saying, his voice smooth and controlled and as calm as a frozen pond.

"I understand you have been . . . assisting me, shall we say . . . while my travel was delayed."

"An interesting way to phrase it," Dex said. "It was unintentional actually. A matter of mistaken identification. A man walked up to me and slipped a pouch of gold coins into my pocket." Dex shrugged.

"My gold," Drewery said.

"Dear me. I didn't realize you'd done anything to earn it." If this son of a bitch thought for one minute that Dexter Lee Yancey was going to cough up all that lovely gain, ill-gotten or otherwise . . .

"I would have done."

"Yes, I am certain you would have. However, sir, in the event . . ."

"I want you to know, Mr. Milton, or whatever you name really is, that I hold no grudge against you. In fact, sir, I am willing to split the fee with you, considering that you have performed the, um, service that was contracted."

"I'm sure that is very kind of you, Mr. Drewery, but I still don't see that you've done anything to earn the fee."

"It would not be wise of you to refuse my generosity, Mr. Milton."

"I've never been known for my wisdom," Dex said with an unfortunate degree of accuracy.

Drewery looked at him. And shook his head. "Do you want to know the thing that I question the most?"

"Yes, of course."

"It is how someone of your innocent look and obvious inexperience could be mistaken for me. Why, you're twenty, perhaps thirty years younger than I. And your clothes, sir. You really should find yourself a better tailor than that."

Dex bristled. "I have the finest tailor in New Orleans," he snapped. Some insults can be accepted as the meaningless barbs that they are. But not this one. A gentleman of Dex's breeding knows clothing or he knows nothing at all.

"Aha! Exactly. New Orleans," Drewery said. "I should have seen it. Nothing in New Orleans, sir, but pimps and whores. May I inquire as to which category you would place yourself in?"

"You insult me, sir."

"How nice that you notice. Too many in this part of the land do not. May I offer you satisfaction?"

Dex lifted his chin. "It would be my pleasure, sir." He wasn't exactly sure that he *meant* that. But dammit, what else could he do? He certainly was not going to cower and crawl before a mealymouthed dandy like this one.

"I am not carrying a revolver, sir," Drewery said, "although I see that you are. I do, however, have an alternate suggestion."

"And that would be?"

With a flourish and a grin of perfectly evil pleasure, Drewery twisted the golden grip of his walking stick and with the slithering snick of steel against a brass ferule pulled a slim and lethal sword blade from it.

Dex understood rather more then what Drewery was about. In face-to-face encounters, damned few men nowadays had the skills to engage in swordplay.

Drewery undoubtedly counted on the superiority of his

abilities. For a man gifted with the blade to face another who lacked that same degree of expertise would give as certain an outcome as if one man were given a revolver to fight with and the other given only a willow switch.

Men in the western lands could be expected to be comfortable with rifle, revolver or shotgun, but they simply knew nothing about fighting with bare steel.

The Yanceys, on the other hand, were not Westerners. They were gentlemen of the old South.

Chance Drewery just might be in for something of a surprise.

With a tight-lipped grin prompted more by grim resolution than any impulse toward enjoyment, Dex took hold of his own cane and with a twist of the grip bared his blade.

"At your pleasure, sir," he said to a suddenly very wide-eyed Drewery.

· 45 ·

Drewery was surprised. It did not necessarily follow that he was inept, although Dex quite frankly would have preferred that.

The man recovered quickly and without apology or preamble stepped into a quick and accurate thrust intended to pierce Dex's bowel and end the affair in short order.

Dex hadn't spent that many hours with an epee in hand for nothing, however. Muscle and reflex took over where eye and reason might have faltered and without conscious thought he parried Drewery's effort, countering with a flick of his wrist that sent Drewery's thrust harmlessly aside and allowing Dex to bring his own blade forward in a smooth riposte.

Drewery's answer, Dex thought, was slow. Effective, yes, but only at the last instant did the man sweep Dex's blade aside with his own.

The first engagement ending without blood, the two circled warily, eyeing each other in the dim, leaf-dappled moonlight that reached the grassy sward.

Dex rolled his shoulders as he cautiously stepped from left to right with his sword blade poised. He'd been tight-pent, and that would not do in an engagement of steel.

Muscles loose and long were needed here, reflexes quick and accurate.

Dex stepped forward, changing the rhythm of his movement, and tried a lunge.

Again at the last possible instant Drewery's blade darted down and to the side, parrying Dex's thrust and turning it astray.

Dex found himself wondering if Chance Drewery's reactions were perhaps too slow, or if the man, older and presumably more experienced than he, were only trying to lull him into a false sense of superiority, trying to draw him in for a killing touch. Or had age and confidence slowed the man's hands and dulled his reflexive responses?

Before Dex could reach any conclusions, Drewery attacked again in a flurry of calculated moves. Step, thrust, block the riposte, step, thrust, block, step. The movement came with startling speed that was intended to confuse and to overwhelm.

It was a game Dex had seen before and one that James liked to employ in their boyhood practices.

For months James was able to overcome Dex's ability to parry, his blunted but stinging blade battering Dex's practice foil in much the same way a saber is employed to, in essence, club one's opponent into submission.

For months James overcame Dexter time after time in very much this same manner.

For months. But not forever.

The practices with James had paid off then, and those lessons from very long ago stood him in good stead now.

Instead of becoming confused and allowing Drewery to drive through his guard, Dex retreated with calm grace, paying more attention to the footing than to Drewery's flailing and inaccurate thrusts.

He gave ground but kept his head, allowing Drewery to wear himself out if that's what he damn well wanted to do.

Dex moved completely out from the shelter of the grove and into the moonlight where both visibility and footing were much better than to be found beneath the trees.

He backed swiftly away, parrying only those thrusts that

he had to and allowing most of the wild stabs to fall short or slide wide without Dex having to worry about them.

Chance Drewery, he was discovering, might have been better off to've chosen only cowboys or bank clerks for his opponents, for the man's training in swordsmanship seemed entirely inferior to the education Dex received back in Louisiana, back where a gentleman was still expected to know how to defend himself with cold steel.

Or, for that matter, to attack when sufficiently provoked.

Dex waited only until he thought Drewery's attention flagged, only long enough for the man to have established a pattern of sorts in this frantic assault.

Then Dex countered.

Instead of continuing to retreat, Dex parried the latest Drewery thrust and stepped into the man's assault.

When Drewery tried to slash Dex's blade aside, Dexter simply lifted his wrist. Not far. A matter of inches only. And thrust again. Not for the man's throat or belly as Drewery was surely expecting but for his wrist and forearm.

Dex felt the tip of his sword meet flesh and slide effortlessly through skin and muscle to connect with bone and grate along the side of one of the long bones of the lower arm.

Dex moved quickly then to withdrew his blade. A man who was truly experienced—and brave—could accept that cut and with a twist of his arm capture and immobilize his opponent's blade while it remained inside his own flesh. Dex had seen that done once. But not tonight and not by Chance Drewery.

The assassin cried out in pain and stepped back, his right hand falling away from the guard position and his sword blade angling downward, exposing him to Dexter's thrust if the killing thrust were made.

Instead, Dex stepped back another pace. He maintained his guard posture but offered, "Will you yield, sir?"

"You son of a bitch," Drewery said. His breath was ragged. The brief flurrying fight had taken more out of him than Dex would have suspected. But then as he'd said himself he was twenty, perhaps thirty years Dex's senior.

"And how am I to interpret that answer?" Dex asked him.

Drewery transferred the sword to his left hand, holding the right at his side now as blood flowed off his fingers to splatter onto the grass.

"En guard, you young son of a bitch," Drewery snarled.

"You're wounded, man. Let it go."

Drewery merely shook his head. And once again attacked.

He attacked wildly. Without any possible hope of success. And he circled insanely yet insistently to his right. Away from his own blade. The way the man was fighting it was almost like he wanted Dex to end it quickly.

Or else . . .

A most unpleasant thought occurred to Dex, and as Drewery stepped stubbornly forward, and in quite the wrong direction, Dex leaped backward and to the opposite side, taking himself well out of the reach of Drewery's left-handed sword and whirling in a complete pirouette.

Damn him. Damn them. There was good reason for Drewery to want to occupy Dex a few moments more.

Someone had emerged from the creek-side woods once Dex and Drewery came out of the grove to where they could be more readily seen.

That someone was coming now at a trot. And he had a pistol in his hand.

Dex had offered quarter. Drewery responded by trying to set Dex up for a pistol ball in the back.

"You, sir, are no gentleman," Dex said.

He closed with the man again. Darting forward. Flicking Drewery's sword aside with ease. Thrusting the point of his blade into Drewery's throat at the base of the older man's jaw.

Damn him anyway.

Dex felt his sword strike home. Through the slim steel connector that now joined them felt Drewery's convulsive shuddering as life and sensibility quickly fled.

He stepped back a pace, drawing his blade out of the dying man's flesh, and Chance Drewery collapsed onto the sunbaked earth and browning grass of the Indian Territories prairie.

Dex wheeled, the sword going now into his left hand as with his right he snatched the big Webley from its holster and held it ready for the man who continued toward him at a run.

• 46 •

"Don't shoot. For God's sake, don't shoot."

Dex sincerely doubted that God gave much of a damn what became of Leroy Anderson's man Carl. But he held his fire, having recognized the voice. "Drop the gun," he ordered.

Carl stopped a few feet away from Dex and, giving Chance Drewery a stricken look, was quick to drop his revolver.

The idiot had been carrying it—running across uncertain prairie footing—with the hammer already drawn to full cock. When the Colt hit the sun-dried earth the shock of impact quite naturally tripped the sear inside the mechanism, and the pistol fired, its noise and muzzle flash immense in the stillness of the night.

Fortunately Dex was not hit by the accidental discharge. Carl wasn't either although Dex was not interested in forming any opinion as to whether that was fortunate or otherwise. The only result of the shot, however, was the noise, the bright yellow flame and a thin, keening, rapidly diminishing sound of the bullet harmlessly ricocheting somewhere off into the distance.

Carl stared down at Drewery. "You've killed him."

Drewery's left foot twitched just a little. "Not yet," Dex said dispassionately. "Won't be long now though, I'd say."

"You . . . stabbed him."

"He was armed. Thought he'd run me through instead. He was wrong. Would you like to take up his cause?"

"Me? No! Of course not."

"Who was he?" Dex asked.

"I, um . . ."

"You came here with him, Carl. You helped set me up for him. It would be a great disappointment to me to think that you and Mr. Anderson would do that for a total stranger." To emphasize his point of view, Dex thumbed back the hammer of the Webley. The sound of the cocking mechanism was very loud in the silence. And if it sounded loud to him, Dex could just imagine what it must sound like to Carl.

"He, uh . . . he said he was Chance Drewery."

"Him?" Dex exclaimed with feigned incredulity. He snorted.

"He said . . ."

"I suppose if he told you he was Useless S. Grant you would have believed that too," Dex said with bitter disdain.

"But he said . . ."

"Fuck what he said. And fuck you and Leroy fucking Anderson too. I come here. Try to do a job of work. Accomplish everything I'm asked to do. And what happens? Some son of a bitch who wants to capitalize on my expertise comes along and you set me up to be murdered by him." Dex shook his head in mock sorrow. "You miserable, toadying bastards ought to be ashamed of yourselves. Both of you."

Dex held his revolver muzzle-upward and carefully took the big gun off cock.

Carl's mouth gaped and pulsed like that of a rainbow trout thrown onto a riverbank, and his eyes were locked fearfully onto every tiny movement Dexter made.

All Dex did, however, was return the Webley to its leather. Then he said, "Bring me that S.O.B.'s necktie."

Carl knelt beside Drewery and reached for the tie. He

drew his hand back with an muttered expression of disgust. "It's all bloody. Jeez, mister, it's . . . it's soaked. And he's still bleeding on it. Jesus."

"He'll quit bleeding soon as he's good and dead," Dex advised.

"D'you still want the necktie?" Carl fiddled with it briefly. Perhaps he thought there wasn't enough moonlight for what he was doing to be seen. In fact he was deftly removing the gaudy stickpin from Drewery's knot. Not that Dex gave a crap. It was one thing to kill a man, more than acceptable under these circumstances, but he had no intention of robbing the dead too. Wouldn't be at all gentlemanly, that.

"No. Give me your bandanna."

Carl offered no objections. He quickly dragged the crumpled and soiled article from his back pocket and handed it over.

Dex grunted and rather ostentatiously used the square of blue and white cloth to clean the blade of his sword before returning the weapon to the malacca shaft. He handed the now bloody kerchief back to Carl, certain neither the gesture nor the threat it implied would be forgotten.

"Tell Anderson I don't much feel like working for him again. He can clean his own henhouse from now on. If he wants a refund he can come and get it himself." Dex hesitated, then added. "Or send you for it. If either one of you has the balls to face me."

"Y-yes, s-sir."

"And Carl."

"Yes, sir?"

Dex pointed to Drewery, whose heels were drumming violently onto the ground in the final throes of death. "Clean up this mess before you go, hear?"

"Yes, sir."

Dex turned and stalked away. But he gave a look toward the spot where Carl's gun had fallen first to make sure the man couldn't easily reach it from where he stood.

◆ 47 ◆

"You look like hell," James said. "Pale. Even more so than usual, I mean."

"You would too if you'd had a night like mine," Dex told him.

"Pale? That'll be the day," James retorted.

Dex filled him in on the evening's events. James whistled and said, "Okay, maybe I would've turned pale after all. Are you all right? Do you want a stiff brandy or something?"

"Already done that, thanks. And I'm feeling much better now. I was a mite shaky during the night though, I'll tell you. Drewery was staying in this hotel, you know. Every noise I heard, downstairs, out on the street, anyplace, I kept having this irrational idea that the son of a bitch wasn't dead after all and that he was coming after me. Or his corpse was. It was . . . unpleasant."

"Sounds like it. Would you like to hear something that might cheer you up a little?"

"I have no idea what would make me feel better at this point and sort of doubt there is such a thing, but give it your best shot anyway."

"You know where I spent the night."

"Jenny or Rosy?"

"Jenny. I'll do Rosy tonight. But as it turns out it's a pretty good thing I was with Jenny last night."

"How's that?"

"Anderson went out somewhere last evening. Someplace for dinner, I suppose, because he didn't ask Jenny to cook anything for him when he got back." James made a face. "She had to go in and give him his beddy-bye blow job, of course. Fat bastard. But he was out of the house much of the evening. That's the good part."

"Just how is that supposed to be good?" Dex asked.

"While Anderson was out, I was able to take a look inside his studio. Jenny is still scared of the prick, and I don't much blame her. He's a real piece of walking, talking shit that one is. And he keeps very tidy records. No wonder she didn't want to risk stealing one of the Penn State bulletins. There are only a few of them and he keeps them organized in a leather folio inside a locked desk drawer where she probably wouldn't have found them anyway."

"I gather the lock didn't deter you as much as it would have her."

"Sure it did. For a good twenty, thirty seconds maybe."

"Where'd a dumb black boy like you learn to pick locks?" Dex asked.

"What makes a dumber white boy like you think there's anything in or on a plantation that us colored folk don't know about or can't get on. I've been able to open 'most any key lock since I was asshole high on a plow mule. Combination locks take longer."

"I'm impressed," Dex said. He meant it.

"Thank you," James answered modestly. "Anyway, about those bulletins. They aren't newsletters like we thought. Not exactly. They're bulletins issued by the school of forestry."

"Forestry? Anderson's got nothing but grass on his place. There's hardly a tree to be found on any of it. What kind of bulletins?"

James shrugged. "Bunch of technical shit, that's all. The bulletins give charts and graphs and stuff like that about fiber densities and different subspecies of hardwoods and softwoods and damned if I understood what all else."

"Fiber densities? What the hell are fiber densities?"

"How hard the wood is, I think. The different varieties are all rated. And there's more about warpage and drying times and longevity under exposure to this weather condition and that. But it's all about wood. That's the one thing I'm sure of."

"Nothing there about grass?"

"Nope. Not one sheet had anything to do with grass or grazing or the raising of any kind of livestock."

"Odd," Dex said.

"And that's only the first half of the night."

"Go on."

"Fatty came home about eleven o'clock. He rang for Jenny . . . bastard didn't know I was there with her, of course . . . and went to bed soon as she bathed and blew him. That would have been around midnight. A half hour or so later there was a knock on the door. A Ki'iwa named Hatchet . . . these Indians have damn funny names, some of them . . . fella named Hatchet told Jenny he had to see Anderson. She told him the boss was asleep, but he insisted. He said it was news Anderson had been waiting for, and he'd want it right away. This Hatchet convinced her to wake Anderson, and sure enough Anderson got up and talked to the Indian inside his study.

"Jenny wasn't there, of course, and I couldn't listen in either, so I don't know what was so important that they had to talk about it in the middle of the night. But I'd bet it has something to do with Anderson's master plan, whatever that is, and why he wants Miz Stout dead."

Dex grunted. James was right. The two pieces of news were intriguing enough to take his mind off his own recent troubles. Intriguing but damned well puzzling too. Even if they were connected—which might or might not be the case—Dex had no idea what they meant.

"Are you hungry?" James asked.

"Yeah. Kinda."

"Well I'm near to being starved. That little Jenny-girl can 'most wear a man out. Come on, white boy. I'll buy your breakfast."

Dex stood and reached for his hat.

• 48 •

"Good morning, Mr. Milton, Mr. Emory," Eugene Duckwing said as they came down the stairs.

"Good morning, Eugene. You look chipper and happy this morning," Dex said.

"I may be happy, but I'm not really feeling very chipper right now. The tribal meeting lasted awfully late. On the other hand, it was time well spent. We decided on a president to replace poor Mrs. Stout."

"I still miss her," Dex said. It wasn't a lie. He did miss her. The difference between his views on the subject and Duckwing's, of course, was that Dex expected and indeed intended to see the lady again. And as soon as was reasonably possible. "Who's your new president?"

"I believe you know him, actually. It's Bob Hatchet."

"The man with the stereopticon?" Dex said aloud. But what he was thinking was: The man who'd visited Leroy Anderson in the middle of the night. There had to be a connection. There simply had to be.

"You do remember him, then. Yes, Bob will be our new leader."

"Sounds like there must have been some dissension

about that if it took you half the night to elect him," James put in.

"Oh, no sir, not at all, Mr. Emory. Bob was next in line. He's the manager of the sawmill, after all, and knows more about out lumber production than anyone now that George is gone to our ancestors. Mrs. Stout, of course, carried on with whatever George started. But Bob . . . he's promised to take us in new and hopefully better directions. Talking about that is what took us so long. The election itself was over in no time."

"Really," Dex said. "I don't suppose you could elaborate on President Hatchet's plans, could you?"

Duckwing smiled. "I certainly would if I understood it all, gentlemen, but the truth is that I didn't understand half of what was said last night. Neither did the old men who opposed Bob's plan, I think. And because they didn't understand it they kept saying we should stick with the old ways." Eugene shook his head. "No forward thinking there, I'm afraid. Old ways indeed. If we all stuck to the old ways we would still be running around in the swamps down in Asha'mingo, and then where would we be?"

Free? Happy? Dex didn't say those things aloud, but they did flit briefly through his mind.

Not that the Ki'iwa weren't free and happy here, he supposed. But it still was reservation land. And the way he understood it from Willie, the tribe had come here not because they wanted to but because a "benevolent" government forced them lock, stock, and barrel onto cattle cars and damned well *made* them leave their Mississippi homeland.

That wasn't freedom the way Dex saw it. Not any more than the capture and chaining of Negroes once made them free and happy in their new, civilized surroundings.

"Thanks, Eugene."

"Of course, gentlemen." The friendly Ki'iwa desk clerk smiled and turned back to whatever it was he'd been doing behind the counter.

Dex and James had considerably more to chew on at breakfast, however, than simply the food that was put before them.

◆ 49 ◆

"I want to go see Willie's mother," Dex announced once they were out of the cafe and back onto the street where no one was likely to overhear.

"Why's that?"

"We need to find out what it is that Bob Hatchet plans to do for this 'new direction' he says he'll take the tribe in."

"You think the old lady would know when Eugene Duckwing didn't?"

"As a matter of fact," Dex said, "I do. After all, Willie got her brains from someplace, and at least half of that came from her mama. Besides, Pilar . . . Willie's mother, that is; I have to keep reminding myself that that isn't a name around here . . . the old woman has been around tribal politics at least since her daughter married Stout and maybe longer. So yeah, I'm betting that we can get some straight answers from her."

"And you think that will shed some light on what Anderson is up to?"

Dex nodded. "I do, James. I think it damn near has to. Willie is dead. At least as far as anyone else knows. And you heard Eugene say Hatchet was next in line after her.

His election wasn't in doubt, but this plan of his was. I'd say it pretty much has to mean that Leroy Anderson wanted Bob Hatchet in a position of authority with the Ki'iwa. There's something Hatchet will do for him, I'd bet, that Willie wouldn't have."

"But this Hatchet is just some fool with a stereopticon," James said.

"You want to hear something else strange?"

"I'm game, I s'pose."

Dex grinned. "I'm gonna go out on a limb right now and tell you without even knowing what's up that Bob Hatchet's stereopticons will help tell us why he's doing what he's doing even if they won't help us find out what. But we have Willie's mama and maybe Pennsylvania State College to help us work out the rest of it."

James looked decidedly confused at that point. But Dexter refused to say anything further until they reached the Ki'iwa president's traditional residence on the far edge of town.

Two days later, at twenty minutes past ten o'clock on a Friday morning, Dex found himself seated in formal discomfort in the parlor at the presidential mansion. Also present were Edalyn Bentgrass—known to Wilhelmina Stout as her pilar—and Robert Hatchet.

Dex looked at his pocket watch for probably the twentieth time in as many minutes. He shook his head. "I'm sorry, Mr. Hatchet. The others are late. I apologize."

"It's all right, Mr. Milton. Really it is."

Hatchet smiled. Mrs. Bentgrass smiled. Dexter did not smile. He looked at his watch again. Then cleared his throat.

"Could I ask you, Mr. Hatchet . . ."

"Bob. Please call me Bob," Hatchet corrected.

"Yes. Thank you. Could I ask you, Bob, if you brought the stereoptical views?"

"Oh my, yes." The swarthy man beamed with obvious and genuine pleasure. He lifted a hardside case onto his lap, opened it and drew out a quite elegantly fashioned stereopticon viewer and a pair of pasteboard boxes that he handled as if they were heavy. The photographic stereoptical views themselves, Dex guessed.

"Could you tell me what you have there, Bob? What views, I mean. I believe you mentioned once that you have views from London and from Paris?" Dex said.

Bob practically wriggled with pleasure. Someone really *wanted* to hear about his passion. Incredible. "Oh my, yes. And those are just to start. Why, I have views of the Thames and the Tower and Waterloo Station. Nelson's Monument and Kensington Palace. I have some from the Royal Observatory. Paris and the Cote d' Azur. The waterfront at Shanghai. Temples in Siam and the Great Pyramids of Egypt. The Tsar's Winter Palace and Mongol horsemen. Oh, I have views from everywhere. Just everywhere. Is there anything in particular you want to see?"

"No, nothing just yet, Bob. These views of yours, though. They are important to you, aren't they?"

Hatchet became sober. "They are very important to me, yes."

Dex nodded but offered no further comment. He sat and waited a bit longer and soon, mercifully, heard the approach of horses in the front yard. Dex rose and went to the window to peer out.

"Good," he said when he turned back. "The others are here now."

Edalyn hurried to the door. When she returned she had James and Anderson's man Carl with her.

"I believe you gentlemen know each other," Dex said.

Carl scowled but offered no denials. Hatchet looked wary now. Neither man spoke.

Dex gave James a look and a nod, and James ambled casually over to the doorway and leaned against the jamb. Dex waited for James to assume his position, then approached Carl.

"I asked my friend to bring you here this morning, Carl, so Mr. Hatchet can hear direct from your mouth what plan your boss Anderson has for him," Dex said.

"Plan? I don't know of no plan Mr. Anderson has for Mr. Hatchet."

Dex smiled. And raised the tip end of his cane to tap Carl very, very lightly on the base of the throat. Not too far from the place where the unsheathed blade within that shaft entered the throat of Chance Drewery. Judging from the pallor that suddenly flushed all the color out of Carl's face, Dex was not the only one who made that same connection. Carl began to sweat. He wasn't as adept at it as his boss, but he did seem to be learning.

"I would prefer that you tell the truth now, Carl. Mr. Anderson hired me to do something. What was it?"

"You . . . I can't talk about something like that, man. Jesus."

"You really don't have much choice about that, Carl. I wasn't asking, you see. I was telling you. Now *spill*." Dex emphasized the instruction by pressing a little harder with the tip of the walking stick. Carl shrank back until he leaned against the flocked wallpaper on the mansion wall, until he could retreat no farther.

"I can't . . ."

"You can, Carl. Or at least you damn well better."

"I . . . Mr. Anderson hired you to kill that lady."

"What lady, Carl?"

"Miz Stout. You know."

Dex smiled, managing to look not the least little bit friendly when he did so, and said, "Funny thing, Carl. There isn't a single person in this room who didn't already know that." He turned and added, "Isn't that true, Bob?"

"I don't know what you mean, Mr. Milton. Really I don't."

"Bullshit." He glanced at Mrs. Bentgrass. "My apologies, ma'am."

She said something in the Ki'iwa language that he gathered was a statement of permission or perhaps forgiveness.

"You knew good and well, Bob, that I was here to kill Wilhelmina. Just like you knew what you would do as soon as you got control of the tribal council. As President you have the authority to enter into timber contracts. Which you are prepared to do next week. I believe your meeting with Mr. Anderson and Mr. Sinclair is scheduled for two o'clock Monday afternoon next, is it not?"

"How did you . . . ?"

"Know?" Dex finished the sentence for him. "Easy. We eavesdropped on you. To be precise, my friend James there has spent the past several evenings outside Anderson's study with an ear trumpet pressed to the wall. We know all about the summons to Sinclair and the contract."

Dex glared at Hatchet. "We also know that that contract would ruin the Ki'iwa tribe. It would destroy the forest. Within two years' time you . . . or Anderson actually because you wouldn't be around that long . . . would denude these mountains of every last bit of useable timber. For railroad ties, isn't it? It has to be, considering who Sinclair works for.

"So you would contract with Anderson and Anderson with Sinclair, and Anderson would get rich and the Ki'iwa would go broke. But you wouldn't be around to see any of that, Bob. You . . . or so you believe . . . would be traveling. Living in fine style on the profits amassed from the ruination of your own people. You would be able to go and see for yourself the punts on the Thames and the Changing of the Guard and the dhows on the Nile. Isn't that right, Bob?"

"You don't know anything, Mr. Milton. This is all nonsense."

"Is it, Bob? Nonsense? No, it isn't nonsense. It is sad, though. Sad that such a dreary little man as you would sell out an entire people, his own people at that, in exchange for the privilege of becoming a tourist. Now that, sir, that is sad."

"And you," Dex said, turning to Carl, "you know what Bob doesn't. You know the rest of it. You know where Bob would really be if his plan ever came to fruition."

"I don't know what you mean," Carl said. But his voice was weak and carried no conviction in it.

"Tell him," Dex said. "Tell Bob the rest of it."

Carl shook his head, and Dex pressed into his flesh again with the tip of the cane. Hard this time.

"He's gonna have you killed too," Carl blurted. "He already paid Drewery here . . . Milton . . . whoever the fuck he is . . . Leroy already paid him a thousand dollars against two grand to kill you too. He already kilt Miz Stout. Then with you dead too come next week Leroy has his contract in hand and won't have to keep paying you off. He won't have to split the profit with you. It'll all be his."

"What about you, Carl? What are you to get out of it?"

"I . . ." Carl looked quite thoroughly miserable. "A bonus. He said he'd give me a big bonus. He said I could kill Hatchet here after . . . you know . . . you and him had that misunderstanding the other night when you killed . . . whoever that man was that said he was Chance Drewery. Sir."

Dex gave him another unsettlingly wicked smile. "Know who that man with the sword really was, Carl?"

"No sir, I surely don't, an' neither does Leroy."

"It was Chance Drewery, Carl. The man I killed the other night was the real Chance Drewery. Me, I'm just a simple country boy from Louisiana."

"But that first night . . . I surely thought . . ."

"Of course you did. A nicely dressed gentleman carrying a cane and a gun. And you hadn't seen the real Drewery before. I can understand how it happened."

"But you had taken the money. You killed that woman. Why, you're standing right here talking out plain as brass about killing that woman and her own mother sitting there listening."

"Yes, that brings up another point, doesn't it." Dex raised his voice. "You can come in now."

A door leading from the parlor into the back of the house opened and a group of old men entered, each of them carrying an ear trumpet and each of them looking decidedly grim.

Hatchet looked frightened to see the elders of the Ki'iwa nation.

But when he saw Wilhelmina Stout walk into the room behind them, the ever-so-briefly serving president of the tribal council's eyes rolled back in his head and he fainted dead away.

⋆ 51 ⋆

"What will happen to Hatchet?" Dex asked Willie. It was the middle of a very hectic afternoon, and they had a few moments alone for the first time since she'd come down from the mountain.

"Banishment," she said.

"No prison term or . . . anything real?"

"Believe me, Dexter, to a Ki'iwa the punishment of banishment is the cruelest of all possible fates."

"Hatchet wanted to be free to travel. Now he will be."

"Oh, yes. But he will never again be allowed with his people. Even in death he will wander alone. His soul will be empty for all eternity. He will think about that when he is an old man, and the fear of it will haunt him when his death time approaches."

"Maybe you Ki'iwa aren't as gentle and kindly a people as I was beginning to think," Dex mused.

"We can be cruel." The girl smiled. "But we're subtle about it."

"You can be subtle in your lovemaking too as I recall," Dex said.

Willie laughed. "Is that a suggestion?"

He grinned. "You did get the hint. Good."

"Now?" she offered, with a dip of her tongue between his lips and a quick withdrawal immediately after.

"I wish I could, but it will have to be later. James and I are going to ride out with some of your younger men to bring Anderson in. First we have to find out who's got the heavy wagon this afternoon. They figure they'll need it to haul all that fat. Personally I'd just take the team and never mind the wagon. Take a log chain and drag the son of a bitch. You *will* prosecute him, won't you?"

"Oh, yes. We have no authority to try a white man, but we can hold him for the federal authorities. I will write a letter to the agency and another to the court at Fort Smith asking them to take over custody and prosecution. Hopefully my letters won't travel all that quickly."

"I think I hear them outside, Willie." He gave her a quick kiss, pulled away but then returned and gave her another, deeper kiss. "I'll be back. Tonight."

"Good," she said, taking a grip on his crotch and squeezing.

"Ouch, dammit!"

"Just so you won't forget."

Dex grabbed his hat and hurried outside to where the arrest party was mounted and waiting.

"Where the hell is everybody?" one of the Ki'iwa posse men asked.

The front door of Anderson's house was standing open. No smoke rose from the chimney, and the place had an empty feel to it.

Dex could feel it. James could too. Dex could see the uneasiness in James's eyes.

The men, a dozen or more of them, milled aimlessly about in the ranch yard, no one seeming to be willing to be the first one off his horse.

No one was in charge, but someone needed to be. Dex began issuing orders. "You two go around back and come in the back door. Give us a few minutes, then come ahead. If the door's locked, bust it down. You, go over to the side there, just in case someone tries to come out a window.

And you, you take that side. You three take a look in the bunkhouse and outbuildings. See if anyone is around."

No one quarreled with the instruction, so Dex guessed he was the one in charge. Sort of.

He looked at James and at Eugene Duckwing, all that were left at the front now. "Shall we?" he invited, and the three of them stepped out of their saddles and tied their horses at the rail in the drive.

The inside of the house had that same empty feel to it, except indoors the feeling was even more pronounced.

There was something about it that made Dex shudder, and he felt a chill as he entered the foyer and beyond it a parlor.

Nothing moved and there were no sounds for several long moments, then there was a loud crash from the back of the house and a voice grumbled, "You didn't have to do that, Henny. The damn thing wasn't locked." "Sorry," someone else said.

Two of the men Dex had sent to the back of the house came into the hallway from a door that obviously led into the kitchen.

"No one's back here," one of them said.

"Jenny ought to be," James said, concern in his voice as he hurried into the kitchen and turned to the left. Dex guessed that would be where the girl's quarters were.

James came back seconds later. "She's gone."

"Not here, you mean."

"No, dammit, I mean gone. Jenny is gone and so is all her stuff. She cleaned it out and took every scrap of anything that was important to her. I mean, Dexter, that she's gone." He looked at Duckwing and said, "They couldn't have heard out here about the trouble in town, could they? Not that quick, surely."

"Bad news travels awful fast," Eugene said.

"There were some of Anderson's hands drinking in the saloon earlier. One of them could have carried a warning," advised a slender Ki'iwa with an ancient dragoon pistol stuffed into his belt. The old gun wasn't capped and might not have been loaded at all, Dex noticed.

"Where is Anderson's study?" Dex asked.

James nodded, and they all clattered in that direction like so many beeves trying to crowd through a gate all at the same time.

The study was massive, masculine and warm to the eye with its expanses of stoned and polished hardwoods.

A huge rolltop desk dominated the room on one side, a sofa-sized chair—Anderson's, no doubt—occupied the opposite wall.

A safe set beside the desk stood gaping open. There were some papers in it, and a scattering of receipts and bank deposit slips littered the floor in front of it. If Anderson had kept money in his safe it was all gone now.

"Looks like Anderson got the word in time to escape," Dex said.

"No, he didn't," a voice said from the doorway. "Not unless he rode out of here on horseback. His driving rig is in the barn. Nobody's ever known him to go anyplace except in that."

"Then where is he?" Dex asked.

"Over here," another voice called.

"Where?"

"Come take a look if you want, but it makes me want to puke."

Dex and James and Eugene Duckwing, who apparently had more sand in him than they would have guessed, followed first the voice and then a pointing finger to the doorway into what proved to be Leroy Anderson's bedroom. The house had a second floor, but if there were bedrooms there Anderson did not use them. Probably could not manage to climb the stairs in order to reach them, for that matter. After all, he couldn't get up the few steps to reach his own front porch and had to use a ramp and handrail just to accomplish that. A full staircase would have been completely beyond his limited mobility.

Not that he would have to worry about mobility any longer.

Dex looked inside the bedroom.

And saw immediately what made the young Ki'iwa sick.

Damn near made Dexter want to heave too when he realized what he was looking at.

A gross sight it was indeed. Leroy Anderson was naked—and that was quite ugly enough in and of itself—sprawled in death on his back, his immense body having fallen back onto the bed from a sitting position at its side. The fat man's legs were spread wide, and the floor between the body and the doorway was glossy with the dark red shine of pooled blood.

Dex had never seen that much blood in one spot. Not even at butchering time back home on the plantation.

Leroy Anderson must surely have bled to death. He was dead, of course. There was no question about that. And the cause almost certainly had to be from the extreme loss of blood.

The thing that made it the worse, though, was the source of that blood.

In the center of Anderson's crotch, where his dick and balls should have been, there was only a red, dark void.

There was nothing there. Whatever the man had had before, it was all sliced away and gone now.

"Jenny," James said at Dex's shoulder.

"D'you think so?"

"She hated having to do that man. I bet . . . I don't know, but I'd bet you that when she got the news that Anderson was going down, she offered him one last service."

Dex grimaced. What a thoroughly awful way for a man to die. Even Leroy Anderson. "I don't see the . . . leftovers," he said.

"And I bet we'll never find them," James said.

Dex gave him a questioning look.

"The girl's an Indian too, you know."

"So?"

It was Eugene Duckwing who answered. "It isn't only *scalps* that we take, white man."

The only thing Dexter was certain about in that regard is that, true to James's prediction, no one ever did locate Leroy Anderson's missing pieces.

But then no one tried very hard to look for them either.

JAKE LOGAN
TODAY'S HOTTEST ACTION WESTERN!